The
Clergyman's Wife

The
Clergyman's Wife

A Pride & Prejudice Novel

MOLLY GREELEY

WILLIAM MORROW

An Imprint of HarperCollins*Publishers*

P.S.™ is a trademark of HarperCollins Publishers.

THE CLERGYMAN'S WIFE. Copyright © 2019 by Molly Greeley. All rights reserved. Printed in the United States of America. No part of this book may be used or reproduced in any manner whatsoever without written permission except in the case of brief quotations embodied in critical articles and reviews. For information, address HarperCollins Publishers, 195 Broadway, New York, NY 10007.

HarperCollins books may be purchased for educational, business, or sales promotional use. For information, please email the Special Markets Department at SPsales@harpercollins.com.

FIRST EDITION

Designed by Diahann Sturge

Library of Congress Cataloging-in-Publication Data has been applied for.

ISBN 978-0-06-294291-3

19 20 21 22 23 LSC 10 9 8 7 6 5 4 3 2 1

To (all) my parents,
for putting books in my hands and letting
me read them at the dinner table;
to (my) Jane,
for inspiring me to try;
and to Stu,
for Sundays, and every day

Miss Lucas perceived him from an upper window as he walked towards the house, and instantly set out to meet him accidentally in the lane. But little had she dared to hope that so much love and eloquence awaited her there.

—Jane Austen, *Pride and Prejudice*

The
Clergyman's Wife

Autumn

r. Collins walks like a man who has never become comfortable with his height: his shoulders hunched, his neck thrust forward. His legs cross great stretches of ground with a single stride. I see him as I pass the bedroom window, and for a moment I am arrested, my lungs squeezing painfully under my ribs, the pads of my fingers pressed against the cool glass. The next moment, I am moving down the stairs, holding my hem above my ankles. When I push open the front door and step out into the lane, I raise my eyes and find Mr. Collins only a few feet distant.

Mr. Collins sees me and lifts his hat. His brow is damp

with the exertion of walking and his expression is one of mingled anticipation and wariness. Seeing it, the tightness in my chest dissipates. Later, when I have time to reflect, I will perhaps wonder how it is possible to simultaneously want something so much and so little, but in the moment before Mr. Collins speaks, as I step toward him through the fallen leaves, I am awash in calm.

ON THE MORNING of my wedding, my mother dismisses the maid and helps me to dress herself. Lady Lucas is not a woman prone to excessive displays of emotion, but this morning her eyes are damp and her fingers tremble as she smooths the sleeves of my gown. It is only my best muslin, though newly trimmed at the bodice with lace from one of my mother's old evening dresses. My father went to town the other day, returning with a few cupped hothouse roses, only just bloomed, to tuck into my hair this morning. He offered them to me, his face pink and pleased, and they were so lovely, so evocative of life and warmth even as winter grayed and chilled the landscape outside, that even my mother did not complain about the expense.

"Very pretty," my mother says now, and I feel my breath catch and hold behind my breastbone. I cannot recall having heard those particular words from her since I was a small child. I look at my reflection in the glass and there see the same faults—nose too large, chin too sharp, eyes too close together—that I have heard my mother bemoan since it became apparent, when I was about fourteen, that my looks were not going to improve as I grew older. But the flowers in my hair make me appear younger, I think, than my twenty-seven years; I look like a bride. And when I look into my mother's face now, I find nothing but sincerity.

My mother blinks too quickly and turns away from me. "We should go down," she says. She makes for the door, then pauses, turning slowly to face me again.

"I wish you every happiness," she says, sounding as though she is speaking around something lodged in her throat. "You have made a very eligible match."

I nod, feeling my own throat close off in response, a sensation of helpless choking.

I AM LARGELY silent during the long, rocking ride into Kent. My new husband speaks enough for both of us; he has an astonishing memory for minutiae and discusses the wedding ceremony in such great detail that I find myself wondering whether he remembers that I was also in attendance. We left for my new home directly from the church; my family and a few friends all crowded, shivering in their cloaks and muffs, outside the entrance, waving as we were driven away. Maria, my sister, cried as I left; my brothers looked solemn, my father beamed, my mother smiled a tremulous smile. My friend Elizabeth's smile looked as if it had been tacked in place, like a bit of ribbon pinned to a gown but not yet properly sewn on.

Mr. Collins's awkward height is emphasized by the cramped conditions of the coach. His long legs stretch out before him as far as they can go, but he still appears to be uncomfortable. The hair at his temples is moist, despite the cold, and I have to glance hastily away, feeling a lurch in my stomach that has nothing to do with the jolting ride.

He is very warm beside me in bed. I watch him sleep for a time, tracing the relaxed lines of his face with my eyes and thinking how different he seems without the rather frantic energy he exudes in his waking hours. There is a tension about him, much of the time, that I did not recognize until this moment, until sleep removed it.

He introduced me when we arrived to the housekeeper, Mrs. Baxter, who is broad and pleasant, and to the gruff, graying manservant, John, whose powerful shoulders are built from years of labor. The parsonage itself is exactly as Mr. Collins described it: small, but neat and comfortable, with surrounding gardens that he assured me would be beautiful come spring. His eagerness to please me was matched by his inability to believe anyone might find fault with his home, and I found his manner at once endeared him to me and irritated me thoroughly.

Throughout the tour, he pointed out improvements here

and there that had been the suggestion of his patroness, Lady Catherine de Bourgh. There were rather a lot of them.

At our bedchamber he paused with his palm against the door. "I hope . . . it suits," he said, then opened the door and bowed me in.

The room was much like the rest of the house: comfortably furnished, if a trifle small. "Charming," I said, and pretended not to notice the flush on his cheeks.

We ate dinner together. I had little appetite, despite the novelty of eating a meal in my own home that I had had no hand in preparing. Afterward, I considered suggesting we adjourn to the parlor but found I could not face the intervening hours between then and bed. Tomorrow I would unpack my books and my embroidery. I would write letters. I would meet Lady Catherine, for Mr. Collins assured me that lady had vowed to have us to tea when we returned to Kent; and I would begin to learn the duties of a clergyman's wife. But tonight—I wanted only for tonight to be over.

"I am tired," I said. "I think I will retire early."

Mr. Collins rose from his chair with alacrity. "A fine idea," he said. "It has been a long day." And to my consternation, he followed me up the stairs, his footsteps behind me a reminder that it will forever be his right to do with me as he pleases.

It is not so terrible, I think after, lying in the quiet dark watching my husband sleep. At my insistence, he allowed me time to change into my nightdress in private. And the rest was vaguely shocking, dreadfully uncomfortable, and far more mess than I had anticipated, but bearable. Mr. Collins, at least, seemed vastly pleased at the end, murmuring affectionate nonsense against my neck until he drifted off to sleep.

I WAKE BEFORE dawn, and for a moment I imagine I am still at home. There is a presence beside me in the bed, warm and heavy against my back, and I think it is my sister, Maria, until it lets out a gusty snore against the nape of my neck. My eyes open and I find myself staring at an unfamiliar wall covered in delicate floral paper.

For a moment, I am held immobile by the weight of all the ways in which my life has changed. And then Mr. Collins—*William*—shifts in his sleep, one heavy arm reaching over my hip, his long fingers brushing my stomach, and I go rigid for the barest of instants. A moment later I force the stiffness from my body, allowing my spine to relax back against my husband's chest. Exhaling the breath I had been holding, I wait for him to wake.

I will, no doubt, grow accustomed to mornings begun beside William.

This is, after all, the life I chose.

Chapter One

Spring, Three Years Later

I stand at the window in my parlor looking out over the rear gardens. From here, I can see William's bee-hives and the flower beds just waking from their winter rest. Gravel paths meander throughout the garden; to the right, they curve toward the hedgerows, and onward toward the lane, and to the left, they bend around the side of the house toward the kitchen garden, and the pen where the pig lives, fattening, and the dusty ground where the chickens peck and squawk.

Behind me on my writing desk, a fresh piece of paper sits ready. The salutation at the top—*Dear Elizabeth*—has been dry for some time. I never feel the quiet uniformity of my life as fully as when I am trying to compose a letter to my friend. Eliza's own letters are full of amusing stories about her neighbors, both in Derbyshire and in London; her life seems full to bursting with her husband, her son, her estate, and her rounds of parties and social calls.

Society here in Hunsford is limited, even by the standards of one who spent her girlhood in modest Meryton. Besides the de Bourghs there is only one truly genteel family with whom we socialize, and though William claims to be comfortable in *all* circles, he prefers to be among people whose station in life equals, or exceeds, his own; and so we spend much of our time at home, and much of *that* is spent apart, William keeping mostly to his book room and the garden, and I to my parlor and the nursery. This does not usually bother me, for it is easy to fill my hours with things that need doing. There is always the menu to plan, the accounts to balance, the kitchen garden to tend. I embroider a great deal more than I used to, and my designs have improved, I think. But descriptions of embroidery do not an amusing letter make.

This afternoon, we are expected at Rosings Park for tea. Perhaps, I think with a touch of hopefulness, Lady Catherine will share some wisdom that Elizabeth might appreciate.

THE DRAWING ROOM at Rosings Park is silent but for the sound of the pendulum clock, which marks the passing of the seconds. I sit, teacup cradled in my hands. Beside me,

William clasps his hands together tightly as if to keep himself from fidgeting, something Lady Catherine cannot abide.

The lady in question is dozing openmouthed in her chair. She has been asleep for nearly a quarter hour. I am tired as well, so tired that I yawn, the opulence that surrounds me blurring into a haze of gleaming wood and gilding. I catch William's repressive glance as I cover my mouth with the back of one hand.

Miss Anne de Bourgh and her companion murmur together beside the hearth, too far away for William and me to partake in their conversation. The fire blazes strongly, too strongly for the warm spring day, yet Miss de Bourgh wears a heavy shawl. Her companion, Mrs. Jenkinson, by contrast, appears flushed from the heat, though as ever she is uncomplaining.

I shift subtly to stretch my aching shoulders and try to hold in another yawn. *Chock, chock, chock* goes the pendulum. I sip my tea, which is now tepid; stare down at the leaves settled in the bottom of my cup; and read the tedium of the next few hours there.

A muffled snort; I look up to find Lady Catherine looking around the room in apparent befuddlement. She slipped inelegantly downward while she was asleep, and now she pushes herself upright, fingers fixed clawlike around the arms of her chair. Her eyes dart from me to William and back again; from the corner of my own eye, I can tell that he is avoiding her gaze, his head tipped back as though he is studying the large portrait of her late husband, Sir Lewis, which hangs on the wall behind her. I return my own gaze to my teacup. At times, William shows surprising wisdom.

"Play, Mrs. Jenkinson," Lady Catherine says abruptly. "It is too quiet."

Mrs. Jenkinson startles, interrupted, it seems, midsentence. Miss de Bourgh presses her lips together and looks at the fire as her companion rises to her feet and moves to the pianoforte, where she sits and fumbles through the sheets of music to find a song.

Lady Catherine makes a sound of annoyance. "I hope your daughter will outgrow her ill temper," she says, turning to me. Her voice, forceful under any circumstances, seems especially startling as it breaks the silence; Mrs. Jenkinson jumps a little on her stool. "Anne told me she could hear her wailing away when she took her drive past your home yesterday."

For a long moment, I keep myself very still. I think of Louisa crying for me as William and I left the parsonage to come to Rosings; she squirmed miserably in Martha's arms as I kissed her head and walked through the door.

Mrs. Jenkinson begins to play, and Miss de Bourgh looks up. Her eyes meet mine just briefly, and then she looks away.

"Louisa has a happy disposition much of the time, Lady Catherine," I say at last. "But I believe she is cutting her first tooth, and it is making her a little fractious."

Lady Catherine sniffs. "Anne was never so disruptive," she says. "Dr. Grant recommended a solution that kept her very quiet; her nurse said it was a marvel. You must ask him about it."

I hold my tongue, actually hold it between my teeth, as William bobs his head, though my mind is filled with frantic thoughts. My eyes stray to Miss de Bourgh, to her hollow cheeks and the sharply delineated bones at her wrists.

"Indeed we shall, Your Ladyship," William says. "Your advice, as ever, is both timely and sensible—"

"Yes, yes," Lady Catherine says, waving a hand, and then she raises her voice slightly. "You play with so little *feeling*, Mrs. Jenkinson," she says; Mrs. Jenkinson's shoulders jerk, and I look down at my lap.

"ROSES!" WILLIAM SAYS over dinner. He slurps a spoonful of soup and I glance away until he speaks again. "Such condescension on the part of her ladyship. I never expected this— did you, my dear?"

I take a sip of my wine before answering. "No, I did not."

There are, we learned today at tea, to be roses at the parsonage. The garden wants improving, Lady Catherine said, and nothing but roses will do to add the necessary elegance to the house's prospect from the lane. William, of course, was gratified by his patroness's interest and made certain to tell her so, at great length.

"And to think," he says now, around a mouthful of bread, "that she even considered the delicacy of the plants—for roses, I understand, are very temperamental. That she has not only purchased them but insists upon sending someone to plant them properly and instruct me in their care—she is munificence itself."

"Indeed. As always."

He pauses delicately, then says, "Do you recall in which spot her ladyship said the roses were to be planted?"

"Near the road, past the hedgerow path." I can only assume Lady Catherine wishes them to be visible to all who pass.

"Ah. Yes. I thought so." William blinks a little too rapidly. Then he shakes his head and dips his spoon once more into his bowl.

I watch him for a moment. "Did you have other plans for that space?"

"I . . . Well." I feel a pang of sympathy at the sight of his bemused expression. "It is of no consequence," he says at last. "I thought perhaps to put a new bed of . . . But her ladyship is very good to take such an expense upon herself, to adorn our humble abode so extravagantly. Roses!" he says again, and slurps his soup.

Chapter Two

I am walking in the garden when I hear them—a rhythmic thunking, a man's voice raised in wordless frustration. The sounds rip through the hush of daybreak, startling Louisa, who had finally dozed off with her cheek on my shoulder. She and I were both awake through much of the night as she cried her distress over her poor, swollen gums until I was ready to weep with exhausted frustration myself. When at last the first tentative light of dawn showed around the edges of the window curtains, I threw a shawl over my shoulders and bundled Louisa into another, crept from the room without disturbing William, and went out into the garden hoping that the cool air would soothe her. As it did, admirably, until just now.

My boots crunch over the gravel paths, my breath puffing warm before me. John, our manservant, is old, half-deaf, and unlikely to hear me even if I shout for him. And I can imagine the way William would stumble about, pulling on his boots and breeches, were I to rouse him to warn off the intruder. And so I hurry along, Louisa keening peevishly against my neck, until at last I round a bend in the hedgerow path and see there a man bent over a pick and fighting what appears to be a losing battle with the immense tree stump on the edge of the property.

I know him instantly, for I have exchanged greetings with him in church nearly every Sunday for the past three years. "Mr. Travis!" I say, and his head jerks up. "What are you doing?"

"Mrs. Collins," he says. His eyes slide to one side; he rests the head of the pick on the ground and reaches up with his other hand to rub the back of his neck, his gaze resting somewhere over my shoulder. "Please excuse me; I did not mean to disturb you."

Louisa whines more shrilly and I glance down at her. And then—oh—the mortification. There is my shawl, damp with my baby's drool, and underneath it my nightgown. My hair, still in its nighttime plait, straggles over my other shoulder; I know, without having to see, that loose strands must be standing out wildly around my face. When I look back at Mr. Travis, I can feel the redness in my cheeks.

"What are you doing?" I say again, voice haughty, as if I

am imitating Lady Catherine. My ridiculousness swells, but I raise my chin in defiance: he is—inexplicably—in *my* garden.

A cough, which, I suspect, is suppressing a laugh. "Apologies," he says. "It's to do with the roses, you see."

I must look quite blank, for he adds, "You *do* know about the roses?"

"Yes," I say. "Lady Catherine told us yesterday at tea. It is only—I expected Mr. Saxon, or one of the under-gardeners. Not—"

"Not a farmer," he says, smiling.

"No, not a farmer," I agree. "Or am I wrong in thinking roses are not generally in a farmer's purview?"

"I am knowledgeable about plants," he says. "My father was head gardener at Rosings before Mr. Saxon."

I should have known this already, and so there is an awkward little silence. I lift Louisa higher onto my shoulder; by the limp way she is draped against me, I can tell that she has drifted once more to sleep. Belatedly, I say, "How *is* your father?"

"Well enough, thank you, Mrs. Collins. He moves slowly, and I—well. I worry that he is a little lonely, sometimes, alone all day. But he seems content, most of the time."

"This must be a very busy time of year for you," I venture.

"It is. Lambing will be upon us soon. But," he says with a wry little smile, "it is a busy time of year for gardeners as well, and apparently Mr. Saxon could not be spared. Lady Catherine's steward told me her ladyship requested my assistance."

"Requested," I say; the word sounds as bitter as it tastes, and I immediately wish it unsaid.

"Lady Catherine is not to be refused lightly." A small hesitation and then he says, "I have taken it as a mark of great favor, that her ladyship has taken enough notice of me to recall that I am the son of her former gardener." His words could have been William's but the tone is sly, and I find myself smiling at his irreverence.

Mr. Travis's gaze shifts to Louisa, and I look down to find that she has opened her eyes and is looking at him with great solemnity, almost the entirety of one fist in her mouth. He smiles fully for the first time, showing crooked teeth. I am suddenly unsettled, and take a step back.

"I—will leave you to your work," I say.

If he thinks anything of my abruptness, Mr. Travis does not show it. "Mrs. Collins," he says, then ducks his head so that it is level with my daughter's. "Miss Collins."

Louisa smiles around her fingers, and I nod, then turn quickly enough that I nearly lose my footing. I catch my balance just before I stumble and hurry up the path toward the house without looking back.

WHEN MARTHA ARRIVES to take charge of Louisa, I pick up my sewing with a sort of shamed sense of purpose. There are shirts to make for the poorer laborers, and caps and gowns for babies whose mothers are too poor or too busy to make many themselves. These are the usual duties of a clergyman's wife, but today I feel particularly driven to accomplish them. My mind churns over my conversation with Mr. Travis as the afternoon wears away and I make stitch after stitch.

"It is best to treat tenants briskly," Lady Catherine said to me when I first arrived in Hunsford. "You have had no experience with such things, Mr. Collins tells me, so you must learn quickly. Vices must be seen and condemned. Illnesses, births, deaths—these require your attention, and of course if they come to you for advice about their housekeeping or their children, you must oblige them. But do not *coddle* my tenants with too much charity or attention, for such things only encourage sloth."

I have lived according to her ladyship's edict for the past three years. It has not, I am sorry to say, been a great hardship; having rarely been thrown into intimate quarters with true poverty or deprivation in my life in Hertfordshire, I found, when embarking upon my new role, that I had no clear idea how to approach the meanest among her ladyship's tenants. I cringe, sometimes, to hear William's tone of condescension when he speaks to his parishioners, but I fear that my own discomfort and pity must be all too obvious. I have been able to justify not giving the parishioners more attention than they ask for by heeding the thought, ever present in my mind, that my family's happiness is tied to Lady Catherine's pleasure. And, too, there has always been the whispering fear that my assistance may be entirely unwanted; that rather than being helpful, I am merely foisting my presence upon others.

Mr. Travis's father is elderly; he comes to church but rarely. And yet I have never called upon him. If I had, I might have known that he once held the position of Rosings's head gardener. If anything, I think with sudden ferocity, my behavior has balanced Lady Catherine's, for her ladyship inserts herself into her tenants' lives, giving advice that might just as well be called orders, just as freely as she does into my own. The difference, though, is that while I find her meddling inconvenient—the last time she took an interest in the parsonage, I lost the use of my parlor for nearly a week while new paper-hangings were installed and she dictated the rearrangement of the furniture—it does no actual harm. But a farmer . . . I hope that her ladyship's steward has offered Mr. Travis wages in return for his help with our garden, but even so, the hours Mr. Travis spent this morning, removing that stump so roses can be planted in its place; the hours he must spend, still, once the flowers arrive—that is all time away from his farm, his livelihood. A farm flourishes only under the farmer's constant labor and care.

I stab my needle into the cloth with too much force, and make another stitch. Our lives are all arranged according to Lady Catherine's whims.

Chapter Three

William refused to hold Louisa after she was born. "When she is larger, dear Charlotte, when she is larger," he said, his hands fluttering nervously about until he finally clasped them together behind his back, bending to peer into the cradle.

My mother came to Kent in time for the birth and remained for several weeks after, for which I felt an exhausted and profound gratitude. I was utterly unprepared for my new baby's relentless neediness, and sometimes in the early days, my body still raw and aching, I looked down at my daughter—an unlovely creature with William's lumpy nose and my own pointed chin—and began crying without warning, hot tears that felt like a curious combination of despair and joy. My mother said nothing at these times, only looked on with sympathy. She ran the household while I was overwhelmed and healing, and for the first time I appreciated that she had gone through this again and again, first with my own birth and then with the births of each of my siblings.

Lady Catherine visited several days after Louisa was born and declared our daughter healthy and robust. She then proceeded to tell me what sort of pap Mrs. Baxter ought to be preparing for the new baby; how many extra gowns and caps Louisa would need, as it was obvious I had not sewn nearly enough; and that she herself had procured the services of a village girl to act as a nursemaid during the day, so that I would not be so taken up by my maternal duties that I would neglect my obligations to the parish.

"Mr. Collins," she said, "I know your income to the last penny. To keep your wife tied to a baby night *and* day is unnecessary, and would greatly lessen her ability to support your work. Do not be miserly, Mr. Collins. There is nothing so disagreeable as a miser. I shall send a girl to you, someone sensible and honest, and Mrs. Collins will thank me for it."

I thought William might swoon with ecstasy.

Lady Catherine's prediction proved correct, however—in this instance I am, for once, deeply appreciative of her meddling, so much so that I sometimes feel a jolt of guilt when my mind fills with uncharitable thoughts during William's soliloquies on his patroness's thoughtful generosity. When

the time came at last for my mother to return to Hertfordshire, I held my tiny, mewling babe, waved at the coach as it
rattled down the lane, and felt as though something inside of
me were dissolving. But for the steady presence of Martha,
the girl Lady Catherine had engaged, at my elbow, I think I
might have closed myself in the back parlor and cried as long
and loudly as the infant in my arms. As it was, I managed to
smile until the coach was out of sight.

I AM REMINDED of Louisa's earliest days this morning, for I
am pacing, once again, through the garden at dawn, holding
her as she gnaws at a crust of yesterday's bread to soothe her
tender mouth. Though the sun is just beginning to rise, the
morning already feels unseasonably warm, and mist hovers
over the lane and between the trees in the woods beyond.

The path takes us past the site where the roses will be
planted. There is no one there today and nothing but an
empty space where the stump used to be. I stop walking,
Louisa squirming, humid, in my arms, her fine hair standing up from her scalp in a frizz. My own hair is pinned in
a knot at the back of my head; despite Louisa's cries urging
me to quickness, I made certain to secure it neatly before
leaving the house, and to don a proper gown. I am suddenly
conscious that there was no need to bother, and I stand for a
moment beside the bare patch of turned-up earth and tiny,

exposed rootlets. They are white and fragile, and I stare at them before walking on.

I come upon Mr. Travis quite suddenly as we each round a corner of the house from opposite sides. We stop just short of colliding, and he almost upsets the buckets he carries, barely managing to right them before they spill their contents completely across the walkway. As it is, the front of my skirt is dusted with soil.

Setting the buckets down, he reaches out as if intending to clean my skirt off himself. Then he draws back hastily. "I find I must apologize yet again, Mrs. Collins."

I shift Louisa more firmly onto my hip and lean down to brush at the clinging dirt. "It is nothing," I say. "See? It comes off easily."

He straightens with a rueful smile. "I hoped that my presence here would not cause you any further inconvenience, but it seems I have once again interrupted your morning walk." He swipes the back of his wrist across his brow, leaving a streak of dirt behind. Even dirty, there is something pleasing about his face, narrow and serious and gently lined about the eyes and mouth.

"Not at all," I say, and then add without thinking, "And it is not *you* who ought to apologize for inconveniencing *me*, Mr. Travis."

I have spoken too freely. Impulsivity is not something to

which I am generally given, and this marks twice, now, that I have implied to this man that I resent Lady Catherine's high-handedness. To divert his attention, I gesture toward the buckets. "What are these for?"

"Soil from the woods, ma'am," Mr. Travis says. "Richer than what you have here in your garden; roses need fertile soil if they are to flourish." He crouches down and pokes around in one bucket for a moment, then lifts a handful of soil and rises. "See here," he says, but he looks at Louisa as he speaks, rolling the soil in his palm with his fingers. It appears to be wriggling, and I lean closer. "The presence of so many worms is a good sign."

"I—oh." I nearly take a step backward but manage to stop myself, though Mr. Travis's amused expression tells me that I have not succeeded in hiding my instinctive revulsion.

"Forgive me," he says. His voice sounds as though he is holding laughter at the back of his throat, and I am torn between irritation and unwilling amusement. "I forget that these creatures are not the daily companions of most well-bred ladies—or gentlemen, for that matter."

The worms writhe in his palm. "Ah . . . no," I say, watching. "Mr. Collins is the, er, naturalist in our household." Though perhaps *naturalist* is more than a bit of an exaggeration; although William is passionate about his gardens as he is about little else, I wonder sometimes, watching the fumbling way he goes about his pruning, whether his efforts would not benefit from less passion and more expertise. But his attention to detail is often astonishing.

Mr. Travis drops worms and soil back together into his bucket. "I should continue working, and allow you ladies to continue your walk."

Despite the early hour, Mr. Travis gives the impression of having been up and about for a long while, his face flushed from his work and his hair standing up all over his head, rather like Louisa's. "I am afraid this is a very recent occurrence," I say as he lifts the buckets. "Louisa is cutting a tooth, and has been waking early—and often—these last few days. I wish that I could claim to be so industrious as to always be up at dawn for a daily walk."

He chuckles. "Well, I wish you happy despite your circumstances," he says, and nods his head politely before turning down the path toward the lane.

IT IS LATE enough, when we return to the parsonage, that William has stirred himself. He is dressed and seated at the breakfast table, his plate generously filled, and he looks up as I approach.

"Good morning, my dear," he says, applying himself once more to his cake.

"Good morning." I move to the tea caddy, only to be forestalled.

"Your gown—my dear Charlotte—"

"What?"

"It is—dirty."

I look down at myself. With the sun now fully risen and streaming through the windows, I can see what was not obvious earlier—pale streaks where I attempted to clean the soil from my gown.

"What if her ladyship should call? Or Miss de Bourgh stop on her drive? No—no—it would not do—please, my dear, change your clothing at once. What have you been doing?"

I replace the tea ladle with rather more force than necessary. "Quieting Louisa. She woke early again."

It does not appear to occur to William that my response does not explain the state of my dress. "Make yourself presentable, I beg you," he says, waving his fork at me.

I leave the room without looking back, though his voice follows me up the stairs.

"Do keep in mind her ladyship's advice on the proper attire of modest women—your cap, my dear Charlotte, your cap—!"

I SIT, WEARING a clean gown and cap, my pen poised to write and my mind as blank as the paper before me. My letter to Elizabeth, abandoned two days ago, is yet unfinished. I have described the ribbon I bought recently to trim my favorite bonnet, and I have told her of the impending arrival of Louisa's first tooth. Absently, I brush the end of my quill across my mouth, frowning at the inches still remaining to be filled.

Lady Catherine has made a gift of roses for our garden, I write at last. *She has enlisted the help of a local farmer to plant them. You can imagine how convenient he must find such an arrangement, particularly at this time of year.*

An image of Mr. Travis—his dark eyes and unruly brows, the wry twist to his mouth when he spoke of Lady Catherine—intrudes upon my thoughts. I pause, blink, but the image is stubborn.

Rising abruptly, I set the letter aside, yet again. Today, it seems, I have even less to say than usual.

Chapter Four

When the quiet of my life threatens to deafen me, I go walking in the woods around Rosings.

At this time of year, the trees are putting out new, tender leaves, and the woods feel padded by them, safe and gentle, though it is still best to keep to the well-worn paths rather than risk the narrower deer trails. I look at them as I pass, those faint tracks to the left and right, little more than battled-back branches and trampled undergrowth, though I make no move in either direction. I am at once eager and afraid to become lost among the trees.

My step is quick today, for it is Sunday and we are due at church. I hold my dress in one hand to prevent it from gathering mud and make my strides long and purposeful, feeling the stretch of each step in the muscles of my legs. I am soon surrounded utterly by shadows and quiet, and my ability to breathe, which felt hindered when I awoke, is restored. Taking in great lungfuls of green-smelling air, I walk and walk until the sun, scarcely rising when I left the house, begins to shine faint rays between the tree branches; and then I stop.

When I look up, all I can see is the great stretch and spread of the trees above me. At my feet, on either side of the dirt path, the ground is covered in soft dark moss and tender ferns, still curled tightly. The delicate faces of spring violets peer like reticent children from around the roots of the trees. Though I am nowhere near as intrepid a walker as my friend Elizabeth, I feel pulled outside on days such as this, when I wake to the stifling closeness of the parsonage walls; to William's snores and his heavy arm pinning me in place against the mattress. In my own home, and at Rosings Park, I often feel diminished. Out here, though I also feel small, it is in the best sense of the word. I am part of the world here, humbled and expanded all at once.

I bend to look at a clump of flowering primrose, white petals deepening to pale yellow in the center, and am caught by a memory—the musty smell of a long-neglected book, and many fascinated, childish hours spent poring over the delicate illustrations within. I used to copy those illustrations, too, my pencil markings fine and tentative at first, though over the years they grew in confidence. I straighten abruptly, my breath a quiet outward whoosh, as though something thumped me in the chest. I stare at the primrose and feel an itch in my fingers.

WHEN I WAS a child, my father was a haberdasher. Sometimes, if my mother gave me leave, I went with him to his shop and sat behind the counter. I felt very dignified and important, greeting the customers as they entered and helping my father make neat parcels of their purchases. When custom was slow, I loved to wander the shop, the floor creaking under my feet in the quiet, the bustle of the village outside muffled by the great glass picture window. I fingered the smooth silk ribbons and the spools of lace, everything so prettily displayed. When customers arrived, I amused myself watching my father at work; a naturally gregarious man, he flattered with such joy and sincerity that hardly anyone who came in left without making at least some small purchase.

I was eleven when my father became the mayor of Meryton and fourteen when he was presented to the king. His knack for giving heartfelt compliments so charmed His Majesty that my father was knighted, and he and my mother returned from London flush with the excitement of his audience and with the pleasure of now being known as Sir William and Lady Lucas.

But then my father announced quite suddenly at dinner one evening that he had found a buyer for his shop and had secured the purchase of a new house for us, larger and more befitting his new title, about a mile outside the village.

"It is a charming place," he said, and looked around the table at us all expectantly. My younger siblings obliged him by expressing delight, but when I looked at my mother, her face was pale and shocked.

An hour later, I came upon her crying helplessly in the larder. "We will all starve," she said, hands clenched tight around the edge of a shelf, her face, usually so composed, wrecked by emotion. Then she turned a fierce look upon me. "Beware men's vanity, Charlotte," she said. "It too often leads them to stupidity."

THE WORLD BECAME smaller after we moved.

Without the income from the shop, we had to economize. It was a strange reality that, having moved substantially upward in terms of gentility, we had grown substantially poorer in terms of ready money. My mother, a gifted manager of household expenses, had from the earliest days of their marriage insisted my father invest a good portion of each year's profits in the funds. The sale of the business bought us our new, grander home, with a little left over, and this, along with the interest from my father's investments, gave us something to live on. But it was not much, and any extra money was saved toward my brothers' future educations. There was nothing left over for dowries, and certainly not for governesses, and so my mother continued to educate my sister and myself in the best way she could, which meant we learned a very little about a few things, and never grew proficient enough in anything to have any talents worth exhibiting.

I came to see my father's knighthood as less boon than burden; though it elevated the circles in which we moved—thereby elevating my own and my siblings' chances at rising still further—those chances often felt insubstantial as wishes, at least for myself and Maria, paired as they were with a lack of money, both for dowries and for circulating us in London during the Season. In theory, as the daughters of Sir William Lucas we might still have gotten husbands possessed of both good breeding (my father's hope) and great wealth (my mother's); but our options in Meryton were few. Indeed, as the years passed and the likelihood that I would make a good match grew ever smaller, it sometimes seemed to me that my sister and I, at least, would have been better served had our father chosen financial prudence over social climbing, for there were many young men in the neighborhood who might have offered for us when we were still a merchant's daughters. But in severing all ties to his past as a tradesman, our father had pulled us out of their sphere and into another, where we dangled, just out of their reach. I imagined their hands, reaching upward but unable to grasp us, while our hands scrabbled for purchase above our own heads; I, in particular, with no money and not even Maria's prettiness to serve as currency, felt my fingers slipping further as time went by.

It is a little different for my brothers, for though knighthoods cannot be inherited, they benefited from both increased marriage prospects and the chance to make their livings in genteel professions as clergymen or barristers. They were tugged upward by our father's decision, just as Maria and I were, but unlike us, they will have the means to keep themselves there without relying upon our father or any other man.

Our new home, dubbed Lucas Lodge by my father, was large and handsome enough to satisfy his newfound vanity, and it came with a small library already intact, shelves and shelves of books that no one, it appeared from their pristine bindings, had ever opened. My father also left their spines largely unbroken, though it pleased him to be able to show off so fine a collection of books when our neighbors came to call. He was also very proud of the pianoforte, for all that it was mostly our neighbors who played it, during the parties we could ill afford to host. But here my mother's vanity, as much as my father's, emerged—she could not bear to be seen as inhospitable, especially when we were invited to parties at other houses in the neighborhood.

Most of the books in our new library held no interest for me, being mainly histories written in so dry a manner that even the most exciting battles sounded dull. But tucked among a few other volumes on various topics of scientific inquiry was *The British Herbal*. I took it down from its high shelf one rainy afternoon, bored enough to try it but expecting little, and found, to my delight, pages and pages of the most exquisite engravings of plants, every detail of leaf and stem meticulously captured.

Our garden at Lucas Lodge was very modest, tended by a man hired in the village for a pittance, but still it provided plenty of subjects for sketching. And though we'd no money for formal training, the careful lines of those botanical engravings gave me some small idea of how to start.

"You are an artist," Elizabeth said to me once from her seat on our garden bench. I had abandoned any pretense of ladylike posture and was kneeling on the ground, my face close to a great bush of lavender, the better to capture the particulars of its leaves. Her voice was gently laughing. "Clearly, you are willing to suffer all manner of indignities for your art."

"An artist would not have so much trouble with perspective," I said, frustrated by my lack of expertise. I longed to have lessons. Sometimes, in the course of a call I paid to this or that young lady in the village, her mamma would insist she bring out a sketch or painting she had recently completed under her drawing master's tutelage, and I had to shove my jealousy roughly aside, that I might respond civilly. But despite my frustration, I amassed a trunk full of pages over the years, of not only plants and flowers but, somewhat more crudely, landscapes, and a few, rather unflattering, portraits of my family.

I HAVE NOT drawn at all since my marriage; I am, in fact, in possession of neither drawing paper nor pencils, and despite the many hours I spend alone, the thought of taking up the pastime again has not once occurred to me. The garden, excepting the vegetables, is purely William's domain, and I've had no wish to intrude upon it; our separate spheres suit me perfectly. And yet. As I look at the primrose, so innocuous, something hungry rises within me, something that cries, *Mine, mine!* I rub my fingers together, the ghost of a drawing pencil rolling between them, and sigh.

Louisa will be awake soon, and she will need to suckle before we leave for church. And William, no doubt, will be anxious about my absence. I look down at my boots, spattered with mud; they must be changed.

I look up again, at the dense tangle of branches above my head.

With great reluctance, I turn for home.

realized, very early in my marriage, that I had been spoiled in Hertfordshire. Our parson, Mr. Johnson, was an aged man, but his sermons managed to convey sincerity of faith without resorting to long-windedness. By contrast, William's sermons are as rambling as his everyday speech, and those most strongly influenced by Lady Catherine tend to meander longer still, as if he is so afraid of giving too little weight to each of her ladyship's points that he dwells instead too long upon all of them. Today's sermon is particularly digressive, and from behind me I can sense restless movement, pews creaking as congregants try to ease the discomfort of sitting upon the unforgiving wood.

The service ends at last, and I stand with William, greeting the churchgoers as they go outside. Lady Catherine, Miss de Bourgh, and Mrs. Jenkinson pause outside the church doors, effectively blocking the remaining congregants from exiting; I make my curtsy and then move aside to allow others to pass. I can hear Lady Catherine's strident tones and William's harried responses, and I glance back; he has his shoulders hunched about his ears as though he is trying to make himself smaller for his patroness's sake. Lady Catherine at least once, in my hearing, has proclaimed that men ought to be more accommodating of women by not growing so very tall.

I look around for Martha and Louisa, and find them standing a little distance away, encircled by Martha's brothers and sisters. There are eleven in all, and Martha, at fifteen, is the eldest. They surround her like leaves swirling in an eddy, each dragging at her attention, and yet still she manages to mind Louisa, reaching down and removing a twig from my daughter's hands before it makes its way to her mouth.

"Good morning, Mrs. Collins," someone says, and I turn with a practiced smile, which becomes genuine when I see that the speaker is Mr. Travis. He stands with the fingers of one hand curled around his father's arm; the elder Mr. Travis squints at me from under the brim of his hat before nodding in recognition.

"Good morning. I hope you are both well," I say. My fingers move as if to smooth down the front of my gown; I stop them consciously, and hold them folded in front of me in a way that feels artificial.

"Very well, thank you," Mr. Travis says. "And you? I hope I am right in assuming young Miss Collins's affliction has passed, as I have not recently had the pleasure of encountering the two of you taking the morning air."

"Oh—yes—entirely passed, at least for the time being, and she has not one but *two* lovely little teeth for her trouble." Louisa has slept soundly since the teeth finally poked through, but my own body seems to have developed a preference for waking at dawn. Most mornings, I force myself to lie abed, eyes closed, willing sleep to overcome me once more as I feel the weight of the covers on my body and listen to my husband's and my daughter's even breaths. But this morning I allowed myself to rise; as I dressed it was with a clandestine quickness, *escape* in the soft thunks of my boots upon the stairs and the click of the latch when I opened the door.

"I am glad to hear it," Mr. Travis is saying, though his attention is diverted by his father, who is tugging his arm out of his son's grip and moving, with a short half bow in my direction, away from us; when Mr. Travis reaches out as though to steady him, his father makes a grumbling protest.

Mr. Travis watches him go, the line between his brows deeply defined. Then, appearing to recollect himself, he looks back at me.

"He dislikes it when I fuss," he says, nodding in his father's

direction. The elder Mr. Travis is picking his way with exquisite care over the uneven ground, one hand raised in greeting
as he approaches a group of other men.

I keep my eyes upon old Mr. Travis as I say, "I have been
remiss," my voice too thin, like a note played poorly upon
a flute. At the edge of my vision, I see the son's head turn
toward me, brows raised, and I cough a little and try again.

"You have full responsibility for your father's care yourself, do you not?"

"Well—yes," he says. "Though he's content, mostly, to sit
quietly or potter in the garden. He is well enough that he
does not require much in the way of special care."

"Only a little extra attention when traversing uneven
ground?"

He laughs. "Yes, there is that. He rarely comes into town
anymore."

"I am pleased he was able to make the journey this morning. Is there . . . anything I can do to help? I do feel . . .
neglectful—I had no idea your father had such difficulty."

"There is no reason why you should. He has been a . . .
less-than-regular attendant at church these last few years, I
fear."

I am silent. He is wrong—I know he is wrong, and I suspect that he knows it, as well, and that he is merely being
kind. As William's wife, my knowledge of his congregation
should be more intimate than it is, and I feel a flush of shame

all along the length of my body. I wish, for perhaps the hundredth time since I came to Kent, that this role I chose for myself came more naturally to me.

"Would he—would your father welcome a visit?" I say at last. "I've no wish to intrude if he prefers his privacy, but . . ."

Mr. Travis's eyes assess me with unsettling frankness, though he says only, "I'm sure he would appreciate a visit, Mrs. Collins."

"I will call soon, then," I say, just as Martha joins us, carrying Louisa.

"If it's all right, my parents are leaving for home," she says.

"Of course." I take Louisa from her arms; Martha waggles her fingers in the baby's direction, then bobs a curtsy to me and another to Mr. Travis.

"Thank you, ma'am," she says, and, one hand holding her bonnet in place, half-runs down the path after her family.

"Does she always join her family on Sundays?" Mr. Travis says.

I nod. "Unless we have an invitation to Rosings."

"That is good of you. Her family must enjoy the extra time with her."

"I believe they do." We both look back at the family as they make their rowdy way down the road. Martha has taken her youngest brother's hand; as we watch, she draws him away from the mud puddle for which he was headed.

Mr. Travis turns back to me and bends down, as he did that first morning in the garden, putting himself at Louisa's eye level.

"I heard about your achievement," he says to her, and as if she knows exactly what he is talking about, Louisa grins, displaying her new teeth; his laughter, in turn, is warm and full and unreserved.

"There you are, Mrs. Collins!" comes William from behind me, and I turn quickly; Mr. Travis's laughter dies in his throat almost at once. "We must get home, and quickly—Lady Catherine and Miss de Bourgh have been gracious enough to say they will visit this afternoon, so we must make haste."

He holds out his arm, impatience clear in his face.

"Yes, of course." Already I am thinking about what we might have ready to offer her ladyship with her tea.

"I expect the roses to arrive sometime this week, Mr. Collins," Mr. Travis says.

William looks around, clearly startled to find the farmer standing beside me. "Oh! Wonderful news, wonderful—Lady Catherine will be pleased, indeed."

"Indeed. And I should like to find a convenient time, once they are planted, to instruct you in tending them."

But William has caught sight of Lady Catherine and her party making their way to their waiting carriage, the remaining congregants bowing hastily, one after another, like meadow grasses in the wind, as the noble ladies pass, and he merely nods distractedly before saying, "Come, Mrs. Collins, we really must make haste . . ."

I take his arm this time without further prompting; Mr. Travis is still completing his bow as William and I hurry away.

Chapter Six

The roses were delivered two days ago. Nearly the moment they arrived, William sent our manservant, John, to fetch Mr. Travis, but to William's consternation, John returned alone. It had been raining for the better part of three days, and the ground, John relayed, needed time to dry out a little before the roses could be put in it. And so we have all endured many hours of William's fussing and fretting.

I have neglected the kitchen garden because of the weather, but this morning I rise, leaving William and Louisa to slumber on; exchange brief, tired greetings with Mrs. Baxter in the corridor; and go out through the kitchen door. This part of the yard does not have the same drowsy quality as the rest; the air is awake with the sounds of the chickens chortling to one another and William's bees humming around their hive.

Only a short distance away, the pig snuffles and snorts its way through the scraps John has tossed into the pen.

A few days, and a great deal of rain, have done the magical work of completely transforming the beds—the early lettuces have proliferated wildly, the spring cabbages have grown fat, and the first tender asparagus heads are just poking from beneath the soil. I crouch and breathe deeply; the air is heady, damp and earth scented.

I am harvesting the very last of the winter parsnips when someone clears his throat from behind me. I twist to look over my shoulder, and there is Mr. Travis, silhouetted by the fast-rising sun.

"I am sorry to bother you," he says; he smiles in apology and holds his hat in his hands. "Mrs. Baxter told me where to find you. I've begun planting the roses, and I was hoping Mr. Collins might be available after I'm through—"

"To learn how to keep them alive," I say, smiling. "Yes, he should be waking soon; I will ask him to come out after breakfast."

"I'm obliged," he says, then hesitates. "Would you . . . would you care to look at them, and see whether their placement is suitable, before I continue?"

Startled, I say, "I—well, yes, thank you." I wipe my hands on my apron, then follow him down the path. The rosebushes were delivered to the edge of the property and left heaped together, but now Mr. Travis has carefully spaced them out.

Each bush is compact, but as they grow I can imagine how they will form a dense thicket of flowers. Mr. Travis points to each, naming the different varieties.

"You will, of course, need to be careful of Miss Collins among the thorns," he says, smiling.

The truth of this strikes me all at once; just yesterday, I was playing with her in the nursery when she pushed herself onto her hands and knees and stayed there, rocking back and forth gleefully.

"She is nearly ready for short dresses," I say. My voice breaks a little on the last word.

He is quiet for a moment, and then he says, "They grow very quickly. Or so I am given to understand."

"Children? Or the roses?"

A grin. "Both." He clears his throat again. "Does the arrangement of the bushes suit? I planted the first few, but it is, after all," he says with a slight quirk of one brow, "*your* garden."

I assure him that they are very agreeably positioned. Most of the bushes will not flower until next year, but one that has already been planted bears a single, nodding bud, still closed so tightly that only the very tip shows creamy white above the dark green sepals. I touch it, very gently, aware that I am tarrying and yet stuck fast as though I, too, am rooted in the soil.

"It was your father, then, who taught you about gardening?" I say.

Mr. Travis nods. "When I was a boy, he used to take me through the gardens at Rosings Park and test me on my knowledge of each plant we saw. He retired only reluctantly from his position; even now he enjoys the time he spends in our garden. Mr. Saxon brings him seeds and cuttings from Rosings."

"But you did not want to become a gardener yourself?"

"I . . . no. I did not. I suppose I haven't my father's artistic inclinations. Farming suits me well enough. And though I am still a tenant of her ladyship, I thought I would have more freedom as a farmer." His tone is gently self-mocking.

My skin prickles with mirth; I press my lips together to keep myself from laughing. Mr. Travis meets my eyes and his lips tip up, just a little, at the corners; then he ducks his head and appears to focus entirely on the roses once more. I find myself gazing at the sun-browned back of his neck, the first knob of his spine just visible above his shirt collar, and have to force myself to look away.

I straighten. "I fear I am no botanist," I say, but I find my mind returning, for the second time recently, to the book from my father's library.

"Do you know," I ask impulsively, "Dr. Hill's *British Herbal*?"

"No," he says, with clear surprise. "I cannot say that I do."

"Oh." For some reason, I am disappointed. "Well. I had almost forgotten about it, but it fascinated me as a girl. I tried to copy the illustrations, and to make my own from the flowers in our own garden—though mine were never so precise as those in the book."

His smile teases. "So you *are* a botanist, Mrs. Collins?"

I remember sitting in the garden with the sun hot upon my shoulders and my sketch pad open on my lap, watching scuttling ants on the petals of peonies. But, "No," I say. "Truly, no—mine was too superficial an interest for that. I merely . . . enjoyed drawing."

"'Enjoyed'?" he says, head tilted, smile turned quizzical. "Meaning, you *did,* but you do no longer?"

I shake my head. "I—hardly know. I seem to have left such things behind me in Hertfordshire."

He nods slowly, consideringly, and I look away again.

The sun is rising quickly.

"I must go," I say, and hope my reluctance is not obvious. "I will ask Mr. Collins to come out shortly."

"Thank you," Mr. Travis says, and I nod.

WILLIAM IS SO delighted to hear that the roses are being put in the ground that he forgoes breakfast entirely. I watch him leave, then pick up the slice of toast, only half-buttered, which he left on his plate in his haste to get out to the garden, and take a bite.

When I have finished the toast, I return to the kitchen garden and stand idle among the vegetables. From down the path I can hear voices, but they are too far away to make out the words, a murmur low as the hum of insects, and so I walk, slowly enough that I can pretend I am merely taking the air with no destination in mind.

My steps slow as the voices grow louder—or rather, as William's voice grows louder, for it seems he requires little response from his companion.

"—three plum trees and two pear," he is saying, "and they are exceedingly fruitful, yielding enough to keep us in tarts throughout the winter months. The apple trees are espaliered, the better to make the most of our modest space, and two are grafted so that we have eating apples as well as tart. I flatter myself that the apples from those trees are as sweet as any in the county . . . though not, of course, anything like as sweet as those grown at Rosings Park."

I have come upon them, now, and have only to step around the boundary of a hedge to make my presence known; and yet, I am motionless, my fingertips against my lips.

"I grow all the usual herbs, of course—they are there, and there, and there—though I am particularly gratified by my lavender, which Lady Catherine, taking a turn around our garden one summer, pronounced sufficiently fragrant. We have five patches of flowers—crocuses, daffodils, and snowdrops just now, of course, and in the coming months foxgloves and hollyhocks and sweet williams just there, and down that path are pinks and cornflowers. My bees make a tremendous amount of honey, and I credit the care I take with my garden for the bounty. My predecessor was not so very involved in his garden as I am; I believe his wife tended the vegetables, but the fruit trees, such as they were, were quite neglected, and there was no thyme planted anywhere that I could find, unless it was so ill cared for that it died. I was prompt in rectifying the situation, and we now have enough thyme to use fresh in season and dry for winter. And of course there are three gooseberry and currant patches, and strawberries near the house. Lady Catherine was very gracious in complimenting our strawberries, which Mrs. Collins served with cake when her ladyship and her daughter visited us last spring."

William pauses for breath, and Mr. Travis speaks with the haste of one who knows he hasn't much time before the opportunity will be lost. "It is a credit to all your hard work, Mr. Collins—now, about the roses; Mrs. Collins said she was happy with the placement, and as long as you agree I would like to go over what must be done for them. They are particularly vulnerable before they are fully established—"

"Oh, I defer to Mrs. Collins on matters of taste—Lady

Catherine was most appreciative of Mrs. Collins's modest good taste when they were first introduced—indeed, her ladyship strongly commended me on my choice of wife, for she said she was glad I had married a woman of sense and humility, who was neither too lively nor too handsome to make a suitable clergyman's wife."

My breath is caught somewhere between my chest and my throat. I close my eyes.

"I . . . ah. I see." I cannot tell from Mr. Travis's tone of voice what he thinks of my husband's bluntness.

"Oh! And we have not even begun—the vegetables, Mr. Travis—I flatter myself that my vegetables are rather extraordinary."

I open my eyes; around the border of the hedge, I see Mr. Travis open his mouth once and close it again, as if in defeat.

"Last year, my pumpkins were *very* impressive, and Mrs. Collins and Mrs. Baxter had much to do putting up beans and pickles and I hardly know what. I want to put in an extra row of cabbages this year—Lady Catherine's doctor is most eloquent on the healthfulness of eating cabbage—and we are still well stocked with potatoes, even after eating so many throughout the cold months. We have not—"

But I step forward around the edge of the hedge and into sight. It was not a conscious decision on my part; rather, I cannot bear to allow William to prattle on any longer. Mr.

Travis turns to see what startled William into silence, and there is something uncomfortable, perhaps even apologetic, in his expression. My face, my entire body, feels hot with mortification.

"My dear," William says, smiling in happy oblivion. "Was there something you needed?"

"No," I say, whisper-soft. "I did not mean to interrupt, I was just so . . . glad that Lady Catherine's generous gift has finally arrived, and I wanted to . . . look at it once more."

As one, we all three turn to survey the row of scrubby bushes. When William and Mr. Travis turn back to look at me, I am in no doubt of the latter's amusement.

"They are a sight to behold, are they not?" William says, however, his mouth set in a smile of deepest satisfaction. Then he says, "How many jars of beans did you put up last year, Mrs. Collins?"

I stare at him. "I—could not say," I say at last.

"Well." William puts his hands on his hips. "I would have thought it well above forty, but I was not, of course, in a position to count them personally. This year," he says, looking at me earnestly, "we must take care to keep better track."

Chapter Seven

It will not hold a curl, whatever I do."

My mother's voice was edged with hysteria. She held a lock of my hair between her thumb and forefinger and looked at Gabby, our maid, who, having been summoned, was standing against the wall of my bedchamber. Gabby looked back, wide eyed and silent; she was no ladies' maid.

I was silent, too, and gazed at my hands, folded together in my lap. Until just an hour ago I had been filled with restless excitement, tapping out the rhythm of a country dance with my fingers at the breakfast table, humming a tune as I went about my work. Tonight I was to go to my first ball at the assembly room in Meryton; my mother and I had spent the last fortnight painstakingly making over one of my old gowns while I indulged in daydreams about being asked to dance by Charles Long, who had brilliant blue eyes and who had smiled at me once in church.

Until she sat me before the looking glass and began curling my hair with the hot tongs, my mother had seemed as excited as I. She always dressed her own hair, beautifully, since we hadn't the income for a ladies' maid. But my mother's hair is thick; when she removes her curling papers each morning, the ringlets frame her face as they should. Mine is very fine; the curl she tried to create hung limply between her fingers. Gabby met my eyes in the glass, and I looked away, feeling oddly ashamed.

My mother dropped my hair and stepped over to the bed, where my gown had been laid out with great care. I looked at her over my shoulder; she stood with her hand pressed against her mouth, gazing at the gown with an expression of despair. "And this color," she whispered. "This color . . . it doesn't suit you at all, how could I not have seen that? But there is nothing to be done."

"Mamma," I said, and she shook her head as if trying to shake away her thoughts. Her mouth smiled, though her eyes remained worried.

"Here," she said, and came toward me again. She smoothed my hair back from my face. "If we dress it simply, but perhaps add a ribbon . . ." She turned to Gabby. "Fetch my ribbons—we need something to complement the shade of Miss Lucas's gown."

Gabby left the room in a rush, and my mother turned back to me. She pursed her lips, lifting my hair, tilting her head from one side to the other. When she caught sight of the expression on my face, her mouth smiled again.

"It will be well," she said, and touched my shoulder. "You will be lovely."

SITTING ON A chair in the assembly room, watching the dancers through the space between the two matrons who stood in front of me, I did not feel lovely. The matrons' voices were loud as they gossiped, and occasionally they glanced back at me over their shoulders, their faces full of compassion.

When we had entered the assembly room an hour earlier, it had seemed to me to thrum with energy and possibility. But now the room felt overly hot, and my stays were too tight, and the music sounded jarring in my ears. Being neither blind nor stupid, I had, of course, realized that I was not the most beautiful of girls; but my mother had never encouraged vanity, and my father, who always saw everyone in the kindest possible light, had called me from infancy his lovely little Charlotte, and so this was the first time that my looks had become significant to me.

I stared straight ahead at the moving figures in the dance and pretended I did not mind being an object of pity.

IT WAS A very long time before I stopped trying to change my appearance, stopped buying new bonnets and gowns in the hope that they would bring out some hidden, extraordinary aspect to my features. My younger sister came out, and I think it was seeing her easy, cheerful prettiness that finally resigned me to never possessing such qualities myself. Maria only rarely had to sit out a dance; her efforts to dress her hair and make over her gowns only enhanced looks that existed already. She is not a great beauty, but her coloring is bright, she glows with good health, and her features are pleasing. I watched the eyes of more than one man follow her at the Meryton assembly, and the knowledge settled over me like a warm cloak—nothing was ever going to make me pretty, just as nothing was going to stop my father from balding, despite the strands of hair he combed over the exposed top of his head, or give Elizabeth's sister Mary the sweet singing voice she was trying so hard, in vain, to develop. We are as we are made.

It ought, perhaps, to have been a painful realization, but instead I felt weightless with it. The constant striving to become something I simply am not was exhausting, and, quite abruptly, I was free of it.

Or so I had long thought.

From the looking glass in my bedchamber, my reflection gazes out at me, solemn and unprepossessing. I stare back; in the flickering light of the candle on my dressing table, I can just make out the gentle networks of lines at the corners of my eyes. I do not think they were there only a few years ago, though it is hard to be certain; it has been a long time, after all, since I paid my appearance very much attention beyond ensuring it was neat and presentable. Now I look at the slope of my nose and the point of my chin; at the way my hair, brown and straight and very fine, falls around my shoulders. My eyes are dark and serious, my brows not entirely even.

Neither lively, I think, *nor handsome.*

The twist of bitterness under my breastbone that accompanies the memory of William's words makes me look hastily away from my reflection. There is no sense at all in dwelling upon my embarrassment, though a thought still slithers, snakelike, through my mind: that William, with his graceless body and snub-featured face, is perhaps even less favored by nature than I. But this is uncharitable. I frown at the top of my dressing table. It is uncharitable, and irrelevant, besides. In men, handsomeness is desirable, but in women it is essential—except, perhaps, when it might detract from their appearance of piety or the seriousness of their work. Dr. Fordyce, whose sermons William is so fond of quoting of a Sunday for the benefit of the young ladies of the parish, is particularly contradictory on the subject of a woman's appearance; we are, it seems, to be at once modest at all times *and* attentive to the emphasis of the beauty with which God imbued us, that we might be pleasing to men.

The bitterness is still there, at the center of my chest, but I ignore it. With quick fingers, I plait my hair so it will not tangle while I sleep. Then, still avoiding my eyes in the glass, I blow out the candle.

Chapter Eight

"Charlotte," William says at dinner, with an air of studied casualness. He pats his lips with his napkin. "I have been thinking—as the baby has been sleeping so soundly at night, might it not be time for her to move to the nursery?"

I set my fork down very carefully beside my plate, objections springing instinctively to my tongue. But he continues speaking before I can voice them.

"Lady Catherine has spoken lately of my duty—*our* duty—to the estate . . ."

"To Rosings?" I say—stupidly—before I suddenly understand his meaning and say, "Oh, of course. To Longbourn."

"Yes," William says. "Her ladyship is all selflessness—for of course she knows that when I inherit Longbourn she must find a new parson for this parish. But still she thinks of us.

And she worries over the fact that we have not yet produced an heir." He puts his fingers to his lips and lowers his eyes, as if in deference to the delicacy of the subject matter.

I could never be so vulgar as to tell him that my courses have not yet returned since Louisa's birth, and besides, I know—from watching my own mother's experience, with my brothers and sister crowded so close together in age—that sometimes a baby can appear before you expect it. Instead, I say, "We have—"

"A daughter, yes, I know," William says quickly—too quickly. I can feel anger curl around the back of my head, all the unacknowledged things between us suddenly large in my mind, but he keeps talking, and I clamp my teeth together, looking down at my plate.

"But the entail," he says. "Lady Catherine is really being considerate of *you*."

Longbourn is a smallish estate, very near my parents' home outside of Meryton. It belongs to William's cousin Mr. Bennet, who is also my friend Elizabeth's father. Our families have always been intimate, and Longbourn is nearly as familiar to me as Lucas Lodge; I can conjure the image of the sitting room—the blue striped paper-hangings; the pretty landscape hanging over the fireplace; the slanting light from the many-paned windows with their pale curtains—with ease. That I should be mistress there, one day, was certainly a consideration when I accepted William's marriage proposal, for the Bennets have five daughters and no sons, and Longbourn can pass only from one male in the family to another. William has, by his very existence, menaced them from afar for as long as I can remember.

Lady Catherine has never hidden her disapproval of the fact that Longbourn cannot be inherited by women. She told me, during my first pregnancy, that she hoped for *my* sake the baby would be a boy ("So that you needn't go through all this travail more than once, Mrs. Collins; I was fortunate that Sir Lewis's family did not hold with all that nonsense and that Anne could inherit Rosings!"). And when my son died just after his birth, she commiserated with me on the necessity of bearing another baby as soon as possible ("Because of course, Mrs. Collins, you married very late and haven't as much time as younger wives do").

When she came to visit after Louisa's birth, she said, "Well, the child is hale enough, but I am sorry for *your* sake she is not the boy you will need," and I looked down into my daughter's round, sleeping face and saw instead the trembling frills on Mrs. Bennet's cap, and heard her fluttering voice rising like a frightened bird's.

"I know she is concerned for me," I say now. "I know."

William nods. "Then we must move the baby as soon as possible."

"I—that is—" But my instinctive protestations die on my tongue. He is right, I know he is right, though a sharp, immediate grief pierces me. Illogical though it may be, I have felt secure with my daughter beside me at night; if I wish, I can rest my hand lightly upon her back at any time and feel the reassuring rhythm of her breathing. After watching my first child's breaths come slower and slower until, at last, they stopped entirely, while I was helpless to do anything but hold him for the duration of his short life, I know that having her near provides, perhaps, only an illusion of protection. And yet still I wish I had not mentioned, just the other morning, the improvement in Louisa's sleep, for William, sound sleeper that he is, is unlikely to have noticed the change without my telling him of it.

Keeping the cradle so near our bed has required quiet and stillness from us both at night, a circumstance that I know has been frustrating for my husband—though he has borne it with surprising grace, his attentions infrequent. It is his right to make decisions regarding our child, and to make demands upon my person, yet he has yielded to my insistence that Louisa remain with me while she was still so unsettled at night. I cannot deny him now, when his request is so reasonable.

"Yes, of course. Tomorrow," I say. My fingernails are blunt, but still they hurt where they press into the flesh of my palms.

William's cheeks are rosy and his mouth is pursed into a small, contented smile.

I GO UP to bed before William and ready myself for sleep, moving with the quiet to which I have become accustomed. Then I slip beneath the coverlet and lie motionless, listening to the wind outside.

It seems impossible that Louisa is mature enough to sleep in a room alone, this tiny being who was, not long ago, so utterly dependent upon me. I ought to be rejoicing; this is, after all, good and natural. And yet I feel I have been hollowed out, a tree ready to fall. I raise myself up on my elbow and peer over the side of the cradle; in the darkness, I can just make out the curve of her cheek and the splay of her fingers. Her mouth is open, her eyes tightly closed. I can hear her breathing.

My fingertips tingle with the urge to touch her, but instead I lie back.

I HAVE JUST finished dressing Louisa when I hear William's voice from the entry hall. I lift our daughter and move to the top of the stairs, listening.

". . . air the room," he is saying, "and make certain it is ready for the baby to occupy tonight."

Louisa is squirming in my arms, and I descend the stairs,

rounding the bend just in time to see Mrs. Baxter bob a curtsy and say, "Yes, Mr. Collins."

William sees me and smiles widely. "I have just asked Mrs. Baxter to ready the nursery," he says.

"So I heard." Louisa makes a noise of protest, and I realize my arms have tightened around her.

"All will be ready before this evening," William says. He reaches out and takes my hand, bowing over it and pressing a damp kiss to its back. Then he steps away, flushed and pleased looking. "What are your plans for today, my dear?"

I have no plans, as such, but the house feels suddenly desperately confining. My tongue shows a sudden talent for improvisation.

"I had thought to call upon Mr. Travis," I say, and in an instant the idea of doing so has gripped me, and I am at once eager to head out and appalled by my own eagerness. "I'd like to see how his father is faring, and to thank him for his efforts with the roses."

William frowns. "My dear Charlotte—I am sure the honor of being singled out by her ladyship is thanks enough."

"I'm sure it is," I say. "But I would like to thank him, nonetheless."

From the corner of my eye, I see Mrs. Baxter's quick, surprised glance, before she turns her eyes docilely downward once again. William looks as if he would like to protest further, but then he glances at Louisa, who has two fingers in her mouth and her eyes fixed on the view through the window behind him. Rather tentatively, he reaches out, touching our daughter's head as though offering a benediction. After a moment, he pats her gently, twice, and steps aside.

Chapter Nine

Martha is needed to help Mrs. Baxter with the laundry, and so, as I take the path out of the woods and across a broad meadow, my decision to call at the Travis farm feels rather rash. Already, my arms are beginning to ache from the combined weight of Louisa and the basket I carry; my chemise clings damply to my back and under my breasts. Louisa gazes about us eagerly, watching the progress of small white butterflies moving among the patches of cow parsley and early purple orchids, startling at the high-above cry of a hunting bird.

By the time I crest the hill above the farm, my breaths are coming so close together that there is hardly any time between one and the next, and I stop, feeling the furious thumping of my heart, and look down at the fields of early crops, neat rows of green in rich dark furrows, and beside them wide fenced pasture. There are a few small, scattered outbuildings, and then the stone cottage, well thatched and surrounded by gardens. Sheep graze in the pasture with their young, and I remember Mr. Travis's saying, when he first came about the roses, that it was nearly time for lambing.

At the thought of Mr. Travis my heart, which had begun to slow to a healthier rhythm, suddenly jerks under my ribs; I heft Louisa and make my way down the hill so quickly that we nearly go tumbling to the bottom. A bean of a boy, of perhaps thirteen, stops and stares openly at me as he exits the barn. I nod to him but do not call a greeting, for, to my chagrin, I cannot think of his name.

At the cottage, the maid answers my knock; she looks startled to see me but takes the offering in my basket when I hold it out. Mr. Travis the son is in the fields, she says— disappointment trickles over me like the drip of cold rain from an eave, though of course, *naturally,* he would be at his work—and his father is in the back garden. She has a quick smile for Louisa but only civility for me, and as she leads me through a dim passageway toward the back of the house, she tells me that old Mr. Travis might be asleep.

"In that case, I will not wake him," I say, and she nods, looking dubious, but leaves me to it, though I can feel her stare; no doubt she is wondering why "Mrs. Parson" has chosen to come at last.

The elder Mr. Travis is resting on a wooden bench in the

back garden, his arms crossed and his face raised toward the sky. Small and knobbled, the sides of his face bristling with whiskers that shine silver in the light, he looks frail and almost fey. The bench sits at the edge of the path, and all around are flower beds, a riot of leaves and spring blossoms. Unlike the stately topiaries and the crisp clean lines of the beds at Rosings Park, the herbs and flowers here are densely planted and appear quite wild, in the way that always seems to indicate great skill and care on the gardener's part. I do not notice the individual plants so much as the beautiful, carefully chaotic whole, the heavy, sweet scent of syringa like a blanket over the entire garden. I breathe in and out, my nerves steadied, and move around to the front of the bench where I can be seen.

"Good day, sir," I say, and old Mr. Travis gives himself a startled little shake, raising his great woolly brows. "I came to see how you are—"

I stop speaking when I realize that he is ignoring me utterly. His eyes are fixed upon Louisa; he shifts with painful slowness onto his feet, then shuffles toward us. I hurry forward to meet him and he raises a finger and traces the curve of Louisa's cheek. "What a little beauty," he says, his voice a little too loud, and clucks at her, grinning with his few teeth. At his words, my breath leaves my body in a great rush.

He backs up again, very carefully, and settles onto the bench, then gestures with a gnarled hand at the empty space beside him. I perch there, setting Louisa on the ground at our feet. She immediately begins a slow exploration of the garden on her hands and knees, old Mr. Travis's eyes fixed on her with unwavering intensity.

"Are you well?" I say, and he looks at me sideways, making a cup of his hand around his ear.

"I hope you are well," I say—I nearly shout—and he hums a distracted yes.

"And—your son? I hope he is in good health?"

"Oh, yes, Robby's well." Old Mr. Travis gestures toward Louisa. "I can just remember when he was as small as that one there."

I smile. "Was he an obedient child?"

The old man releases a wheeze of a laugh. "Not a bit."

I laugh as well, and then the conversation dwindles, though I attempt, more than once, to engage him. But really, I cannot wish otherwise, for old Mr. Travis has his attention fixed utterly upon Louisa—he leans forward, the better to watch her, palms upon his knees, the spiderweb of lines on his face pulled tight as he smiles. Louisa pauses in her explorations before a towering syringa and looks up, up, up at it. Honeybees dart from blossom to blossom.

"Your garden is so lovely, Mr. Travis," I say.

He looks around us as though assessing his own work. "It's not so easy to keep up with as it was just a few years ago," he says at last, chewing over each word slowly.

"Your efforts are—well, the results are extraordinary. I have never seen a happier place."

Genuine pleasure fills his face, and I look down at my lap.

HE INSISTS ON walking us to the front gate, and so we are making a slow progress around the side of the cottage when Mr. Travis finds us.

"Young Henry told me he saw you arrive," he says in greeting.

I stolidly ignore the little burst of gladness under my breastbone. "I came to visit your father," I say, nodding to the older man. "And to thank you."

"Thank me?"

"Yes, of course." To his father, I say, "Mr. Collins and I are greatly indebted to your son for his work in our garden."

Old Mr. Travis nods. "Robby's a good lad," he says. "A good lad."

Mr. Travis wears an odd grimace, as if torn between embarrassment and pleasure.

"I left some of Mr. Collins's honey with your maid," I say. The jar, with its contents golden and stickily tempting, was the best offering I could think of quickly.

"Thank you," Mr. Travis says, and we stand looking at one another over the fence. He is dressed for work—his boots are filthy—and his hands, resting upon the fence rail, have dirt under their nails and embedded in the lines of his fingers.

Though he is neither tall nor broad, his hands are large and square, his fingers too big for the rest of him. Dark hair curls along his wrists. They could never, I think with an odd spasm, be mistaken for the hands of a gentleman. I have not had occasion to really look at a farmer's hands before; perhaps they are all like his, thick with muscle and roughly callused. I am at once fascinated and repulsed; I wonder—the thought songbird quick, though the shock of it lingers—how different they might feel to William's soft palms. My mind fills with a low hum.

Seeing the direction of my gaze, his hands curl into fists, before he unclenches them again with deliberate slowness. Disconcerted, I press my cheek against my daughter's thin curls.

Old Mr. Travis tickles Louisa under her chin, startling a high, happy sound from her.

"Bring this little darling again soon," he says.

I promise to do so, and we say our good-byes.

We have crested the hill when I hear running footsteps behind us, and Mr. Travis overtakes us moments later. "Mrs. Collins," he says; he breathes hard and lifts his hat to cool his head. "I am sorry—I ought to have offered immediately— might I carry Miss Collins for you?"

I blink away my startlement. "I—thank you." Louisa has fallen asleep, her head heavy on my shoulder, but he takes her from me very gently, and she scarcely stirs.

"She's a hardy girl," he says, quiet voiced.

"That she is."

"It was kind of you to bring her—I have not seen my father so animated in a long while."

"Please—think nothing of it. In truth, she was . . . helpful to me."

He looks at me over Louisa's head, lifts a brow. I strive for lightness. "I rather thought I would be . . . better at this," I say. "It may surprise you to know that this—role—that being a clergyman's wife—does not come naturally to me. It seems Louisa can make a useful bridge when I do not know what to say."

I cannot fathom what made me speak so, and fall silent.

"Mrs. Collins," Mr. Travis begins, but Louisa makes a keening noise of protest in her sleep, and he presses his lips closed, smiling at me above her head. We are silent the rest of the way to the parsonage, though from time to time he darts glances at me, quick as minnows; I know, because I am doing the same.

When we reach the lane, I have to force myself to keep walking. Though there is no true impropriety, I suddenly feel that I cannot face William's—or worse, Lady Catherine's— seeing us walking together. But we reach the parsonage gate unobserved.

"I can take her from here," I say.

"Of course." Mr. Travis holds the back of Louisa's head

gently as he moves her between us; she tucks her face into the crook of my neck, and I put my hand up to her head as he takes his away. Our fingers brush, just briefly; Louisa grizzles against my shoulder; I make a shushing noise until she quiets.

"Thank you," I say, and he blinks as though he has been taken out of his thoughts.

He touches his hat. "Entirely my pleasure, Mrs. Collins."

I pause before going through the gate. "Are there other members of the congregation, do you think, who might not need or—or *want* charity, but who might enjoy being called upon, now and again?"

He is quiet for a moment, thinking. "Mrs. Fitzgibbon," he says at last. "She is—"

"A widow," I say quickly, interrupting him in my eagerness to prove that I am not entirely ignorant of my husband's congregation. Then I blush. "Forgive me, continue."

He laughs softly. "Yes, she is a widow, and childless. Her husband died before you came here, I think, but he was . . . not well liked. I do not know Mrs. Fitzgibbon well, myself, but she has always seemed rather solitary."

I nod. "Thank you." And then, on impulse: "I was wondering—do you think your father would like a cutting from our roses?"

A faint smile. "I'm sure he would. But it would be better to wait until autumn to take the cutting."

"Oh. I did not know." I feel oddly rejected, my gladness dissipating.

He bows and turns to make the walk back to his farm. But then he looks behind him again, at me. "May I say," he says, "you are far more natural in your role than you give yourself credit for."

I hold Louisa tightly as I walk through the garden, and stand there in the sunlight a little while before going into the house.

Despite my misgivings, Louisa goes to sleep easily in the nursery. I leave the door open just a bit so that I might hear her if she cries out in the night. My fingers linger on the door frame, and I bend my head toward the door, listening—but there is only silence.

At last, I turn away and walk the few steps down the hall to my own chamber, and leave that door ajar as well.

I have just settled into bed when the door creaks open and William enters the room. I left no candle burning, and in the darkness he is but a shadowy figure, tall and heavy. I watch as he removes his coat but close my eyes when his fingers go to the fastenings on his shirt, its whiteness muted by the room's shadows. There is the rustle of fabric as he undresses, and again as he dons his nightshirt, and then the mattress dips under his weight as he settles in beside me.

We lie together for a moment in silence. He did not ask

me anything about my day when we dined together this evening, instead talking at length about his labors in the garden and how greatly they tired him, and I think now, briefly, that William might drift off to sleep. But then he rolls over and puts one hand, just lightly, on my shoulder, the tips of his fingers touching my collarbone. I open my eyes. He is gazing at me, his face very close, and then he leans down and kisses my mouth. I feel the chapped skin of his lips and taste the sour tang of the tea he drank after dinner, as well as something else, a sickly-sweet flavor that is uniquely William. He rolls atop me, and his weight makes it hard to draw a full breath.

I am quiet as he fumbles between us and squeeze my eyes closed when I feel the press of him against me. Then, for several minutes, there is nothing but sensation—his chin, sharp with a day's worth of whiskers, abrading my own; the hot puff of his breath against my neck—and quiet sounds. The bed creaks along with his erratic movements; our bodies slap together, muffled only by our nightclothes, which are rucked up between us. Outside, crickets sing.

When he is through I pull the quilt up to my chin. But sleep will not come; I stare into the darkness for several minutes, trying to relax my body and still my thoughts. I wonder how Louisa is sleeping in the nursery.

Then William's voice drifts across the space between us, low and slurred as he nears sleep. "We might have made an heir for Longbourn just now. That would please Lady Catherine." He brushes his knuckles along my arm, then rolls over. Moments later, he is snoring.

I imagine myself rising, moving toward the washbasin. Scrubbing at the insides of my thighs with a damp cloth until they burn from the friction. But I do not. I shift uncomfortably away from the cooling damp that has spread across the sheet beneath me and wait for sleep to come.

Chapter Ten

Mrs. Fitzgibbon sets my usual cup before me at her scrubbed wood table. Made of china so delicate it is nearly translucent, the cup is patterned with ivy and filled with very weak tea. She told me during my first visit that it is the only remaining piece from a set that belonged to her mother, and it is much finer than the sturdy cups and saucers she has for everyday use. Though I am not prone to clumsiness, I am especially careful when I take tea here.

Today I have brought Louisa with me, and the baby—now in short petticoats for several weeks—takes delight in exploring the cramped little room. When she finds Mrs. Fitzgibbon's work basket, the elderly woman merely laughs and removes the packet of needles.

I protest, reaching out to pick my daughter up. "Oh, no—she will make a mess of it."

"Thread can be untangled," Mrs. Fitzgibbon says, and I subside, looking on as she watches Louisa, her smile deepening the wrinkles about her eyes and mouth. She is a wisp of a woman, with white hair like dandelion seeds and a bent and bony figure. She has been destitute since her husband's death, living on what she grows in her kitchen garden and charity from Rosings Park. She has no cake to offer but pushes a plate of bread and preserves toward me with proud insistence.

"I have not had an opportunity to just sit and watch a baby play since my nephew was small, and that was nearly thirty years ago, now." Mrs. Fitzgibbon chews her own bread slowly, and her tongue darts out to lick a drip of preserves from the corner of her mouth. "Only one of my own babes lived more than a week. It makes me feel quite young, having this clever girl to dote upon."

Old Mr. Travis said something remarkably similar just yesterday, when Louisa and I called at the farm. "She makes me forget about my aches," he said. "If my son would only marry and give me grandbabies, I'd probably live forever."

The son in question, who had come into the back garden for a few minutes away from his labors, merely rolled his eyes to the treetops.

"How many children did you have?" I ask Mrs. Fitzgibbon now.

She does not take her eyes from Louisa. "Six," she says. "May they rest."

I swallow. "Louisa's grandmother lives fifty miles away and cannot spoil her as much as she'd like," I say at last. "So you may dote on her as much as you choose."

Louisa tips the basket over so thread, squares of fabric, and buttons tumble together onto the floor. She looks at us and smiles as if she just did something hugely clever.

MRS. BAXTER, LOOKING a little harried, meets us at the door when Louisa and I return to the parsonage. "Lady Catherine has come to call," she says. "Mr. Collins has been asking after you."

"How long has she been here?" I say. "And where is Martha?" I remove my bonnet and touch my cap to make sure it is straight.

"Not long," the housekeeper says. She reaches out to take Louisa from my arms. "Martha and I were cleaning the carpets—I will give Louisa to her now."

I am already making for the front parlor. From behind the closed door, I can hear the muffled sound of Lady Catherine's voice. "Tea?" I say, looking back at Mrs. Baxter.

"Yes, ma'am. And cakes, the lemon ones her ladyship prefers."

"Thank you, Mrs. Baxter."

I pause to smooth my gown and inspect my hem to ensure it is not too dusty from my walk. When I open the parlor door, I find Lady Catherine ensconced in one chair and William perched across from her on another, his body positively humming with anxiety. He leaps to his feet when I enter, clapping his hands together with an expression of clear relief.

"My dear! Where have you been? As you see, her ladyship has paid us the compliment of a visit—"

I curtsy to Lady Catherine. "I apologize for not being here to receive you, Your Ladyship."

Lady Catherine sniffs but otherwise does not appear unduly put out. I sit down, and William does likewise. "I came to speak with Mr. Collins about Sunday's sermon," she says. "Last week's was rather . . . uninspiring."

"I must again humbly beg Your Ladyship's pardon," William says. He is leaning forward in his chair, his eyes so wide that they bulge in their sockets. I look away, pity and disgust mingling in my belly, and take up my whitework, careful to hold the needle in the manner in which her ladyship previously advised I should.

It is easy to ignore most of the conversation and keep my eyes on my stitches, until at last Lady Catherine turns her attention to me, cutting William off midsentence.

"And where have you been today, then, Mrs. Collins?" she asks. She takes a bite of cake and looks at me expectantly.

I glance at William, who has drawn back into his chair and is staring down at his hands, which are gripping his knees. Then I look back at Lady Catherine. "I have been visiting one of your tenants, Your Ladyship—Mrs. Fitzgibbon."

Lady Catherine squints. "Ah, yes—her husband ran the little farm that borders the Clifton estate."

"I rather think, from what Mrs. Fitzgibbon intimated, that *she* was more responsible for running the farm than was her husband," I say.

"He was a drunkard," Lady Catherine says, as blunt as ever. "If he had not had the good sense to marry an active, resourceful woman, he would have lost the tenancy years ago." She frowns. "She did not have a complaint about her new cottage, I hope? I saw it myself before she took residence, it was very cozy."

"No, she is—very content with her home. She was only feeling a little low in spirits."

Her ladyship's brows arch. "Low in spirits?"

"Yes, she is very alone in the world."

"Well. There is no call for her to have troubled you with *that*. If she feels so, she merely wants occupation. If she were to work harder, there would be no time in the day for being lonely."

I straighten my shoulders. "I . . . She did not trouble me, Your Ladyship. I thought she seemed rather . . . solitary. That she might like companionship, occasionally."

"Companionship!" William says in a burst. Lady Catherine and I both look at him, and he smiles fawningly at her. "My dear—as her ladyship has only just said—"

"She has no one," I say, and the hardness of my voice

startles me. I take a breath to get myself under regulation. "She has only a sister, who lives nearly a hundred miles away. There is no one here in whom she can confide." William opens his mouth to say something else and I add, "You were so kind, Lady Catherine, in finding Martha, that I might have time to perform my duties to the parish, and I would not like to shirk those duties. I believe I will take Mrs. Fitzgibbon some paper and ink, when next I visit; I think she would like to send her sister a letter." I sit back and raise my teacup to hide my face. I feel flushed and triumphant, in a very small way.

The look Lady Catherine bestows upon me puts me in mind of the looks she used to give Elizabeth, when my friend dared to speak her true thoughts to her ladyship upon visiting me in the early days of my marriage. Then she says, with great deliberation, "Just so long as you are not encouraging idleness, Mrs. Collins." And, turning back to William, "You must add something about the sin of idleness to your sermon. The virtue of hard work cannot be overemphasized; the poor too often neglect to feel gratitude as they ought."

William is quick to acknowledge the wisdom of her ladyship's words. I bend my head once more to my needlework as the conversation continues without me, much as a stream will flow heedlessly around a stone.

Chapter Eleven

When I was seven years old, I went with my mother to call upon her friend Mrs. Bennet, who had recently given birth to a second daughter. My mother instructed me to play quietly with Jane, the elder Bennet sister, though I did catch a short glimpse of the infant, who had a healthy wail and round red cheeks, and whom her mother had named Elizabeth.

For a very long time, Elizabeth Bennet remained in my mind merely one of the many Bennet girls—there are five in all, the final three born in quick and disappointing succession—all of whom are several years my junior, closer in age to my sister, Maria, than they are to me. My mother and Eliza's liked to visit one another frequently, and generally we children were brought along, as well, for it was a short, easy walk down the dusty lane between the two houses. My mother thought Lizzy was wild and needed discipline, for she spent most of her childhood looking more like a village waif than a young lady of quality, her hair tangled, her slippers splashed with mud. As we all grew up, I spent more time conversing with our mothers than I did with Elizabeth and her sisters; the difference in our ages seemed like a chasm between us when I was of an age to come out in society and Lizzy was still losing her hair ribbons and tearing holes in her stockings.

But when she was fifteen, we happened upon one another at the circulating library, both in search of the same novel. I happened to arrive half an hour earlier than Elizabeth and had curled on a chair in the little reading room, the first volume open in my lap.

"It was *you*," she said, in a tone of laughing annoyance.

Startled out of my absorption, my head jerked up. Eliza had begun by then to dress herself with more care, though still the curls of her hair were a little blown and wild, as though she had run rather than walked into the village. She stood before me, hands on hips, her bonnet dangling down her back by its ribbons. Nodding at the book, she said, "The clerk told me someone had only just borrowed it."

"I'm sorry," I said.

"You are forgiven." She smiled. "Only, you *must* tell me the moment you have finished."

I WAIT NOW in the stuffy confines of the Hunsford circulating library. In front of me two young ladies are giggling together over something in the book they hold between them. They put me strongly in mind of my younger self and Elizabeth Bennet, for after that first chance meeting, we began to go to the circulating library together, and when we both wanted the same book we would take turns reading it aloud. We also passed novels back and forth between our two houses, urging one another to finish quickly so that we could discuss them. The girls before me seem to be deciding which of them will borrow the book first, and the clerk, who really ought to have finished with them by now, is indulging them so that I suspect he wishes to pay one or the other special attention. I cover a smile and look out the window at the people passing outside.

The door opens behind me; when I turn to look, I am startled to find Mr. Travis in the doorway, and though he looks as surprised as I feel, he is smiling at me. After a moment, he walks closer, stepping carefully into line behind me.

"Well met, Mrs. Collins," he murmurs.

"Good day, Mr. Travis. What brings you here?"

His eyes slide to one side. "I am in need of a new pair of boots; am I in the wrong place?"

I smile. "You are indeed, sir."

An exaggerated sigh. "Ah, well. I suppose I shall have to make do with a book instead."

We are interrupted by the young ladies' departure and the clerk leaning slightly over his desk to catch my attention.

"And how can I help you, madam?" he says. I walk to the counter and make my selection, all the while feeling Mr. Travis's presence a little behind me. I nod when I pass him on my way out, and he tips his hat.

I'VE NO OTHER business in the village today, but still I am reluctant to leave just yet. I pause at the milliner's, leaning close to peer at the window display, pretending—for whose benefit, I don't know—that I am interested in a new bonnet.

Only a few steps away is the circulating library. My thoughts drift toward the man inside, and I jerk them away, back to the hats in the window before me. My reflection in the glass gazes back at me, blurry and indistinct—a fool of a matron in a green dress, the lace of her cap showing under her plain straw bonnet. She looks as bemused as I feel, as if she, too, finds the idea of dawdling in the street, hoping for a few snatched moments of conversation, as peculiar and pathetic as I do.

But the door to the library is opening, and Mr. Travis is coming through it, a book tucked under his arm and an abstracted expression upon his face. I turn my head so that I am not caught looking, the side of my bonnet hiding my face. I stare fixedly at an arrangement of ostrich plumes, even as I see his approach reflected in the glass.

"Are you reading something improving?"

I turn. "Not at all, though I shouldn't admit it." I hold my book out for him to see.

He leans forward and examines it, turning it open to the title page. "A novel?" he says, something teasing about his tone. "You're right, you should not admit to it."

"Fordyce's *Sermons* was unavailable."

He laughs outright, head back and throat exposed above his neckcloth, and I am shocked by my own pleasure.

"You do not have your own copy? For shame, Mrs. Collins!"

"No, I confess we do. Mr. Collins has always been an admirer of Mr. Fordyce. Louisa will no doubt learn his sermons off by heart when she is older."

"Like her mother did before her?"

"Oh. Well. I cannot say I am as well versed as that. *My* father is not a clergyman; he is more concerned with . . . earthly matters than spiritual."

"I suppose," he says slowly, dryly, "this is actually rather . . . apt." He looks at me again, brows raised. "*Patronage, Volume One?*"

Dismay rises inside of me, and then our eyes meet and I see his quiet amusement—and suddenly I am laughing, loud and gasping, as helpless against the force of it as a rowboat against a gale. I clap one hand over my mouth and snort through my fingers. The sound is utterly impolite, and from the corner of my eye I see Mr. Travis pressing his own fingers over the grin spreading across his face.

Passersby cast us curious glances, and the sounds of the village around us intrude upon me suddenly—the clop of a horse and cart is loud enough to startle; the laughter of small children racing each other down the other side of the street, and a woman's voice shouting after them, make me flinch. Doors open and then close again; one young man calls across the road to another. I draw in a shaky breath, struggling to gain control of myself.

At last, I turn back to Mr. Travis to find him watching me. We look at each other and I feel my cheeks drawing up, my mouth stretching, and though I bite my lip I am incapable of stopping the puff of laughter that escapes me. Every line about Mr. Travis's eyes and mouth stands out as he chuckles and looks briefly away.

"Forgive me," he says at last. "I should not have said that."

"And I should not have laughed," I say.

He pinches his lips together, as if trying to contain his smile, and just looks at me, shaking his head.

I glance at the book he holds. "And you? Shall I assume your choice is not frivolous? In my experience, men rarely appreciate novels as women do."

He looks down, almost as if surprised to discover that there is a volume in his hands. "It is not for me," he says at last, without looking up.

"It is something your father requested?"

He rubs the back of his neck. "No. It is—well." He holds the book out for me to see, his face closed as winter shutters.

"*The British Herbal,*" I read aloud. "*An history of plants and trees, natives of Britain, cultivated for use, or raised for beauty.*" I stare at the title for a moment longer, then look up at Mr. Travis, uncomprehending. "My father has this same book," I say.

He draws it back from me. "Ah—yes."

I cannot make sense of my conclusions, and I stand dumb, staring at him.

After a moment, he grimaces and says, "I apologize—it was presumptuous. It is only—you spoke about it with so much animation. I suppose that is why the name stayed with me."

I am full of bafflement and fear and wonder, all at once. "You remembered that?"

Another pause, longer this time, as if he is choosing his words carefully, but at last he merely rubs his neck again. "It stayed with me," he says once more, and holds the book out to me.

I take it, and it is as if the shutters over his expression have been pulled back to let in the sunlight. His hands hang down, relaxed and open.

"I think I will go back," he says, indicating the library. "I rather feel I've something to prove, now you've said you think men do not much care for novels."

I wonder who these novel-reading men are; except for Elizabeth's father, Mr. Bennet, I cannot think of any men I know who read for pleasure. "Do they?" I say. "Do you?"

"Mmm. Well. Sometimes." He huffs a laugh when I look at him sideways. "My father likes to be read to occasionally, of an evening, but his taste runs more toward histories. I rarely have time to read for my own pleasure; I hardly know what I would choose. But certainly there are many men who *do* read novels. Indeed, a great many novels are *written* by men; it seems reasonable to assume that other men read them."

"Other than Mr. Collins and my father, I suppose I have rarely had occasion to discuss such things with the men of my acquaintance," I say. "My eldest brother is at Oxford; I assume he must read a great deal more than he did while he was at home."

Something flickers in Mr. Travis's expression, and all at once the easiness of our exchange is gone. I stand, baffled by the sudden tension.

But when he speaks, it is lightly. "I myself have never left Kent, so perhaps I—and those like me—have more reason to seek the escape of novels than do more . . . worldly men."

My mouth opens, but the words are caught at the back of my throat, and before I can force them out Mr. Travis bows. "I wish you enjoyment in your reading," he says. "I have some business to attend to."

I curtsy and say my good-byes and watch him go; he jams

his hat onto his head and dashes out into the street without looking, nearly colliding with another man before nodding quickly in apology and disappearing down the street.

WHEN I RETURN home, I am relieved to find no one immediately about; the door to William's book room is closed, and I can hear, softly, Martha singing upstairs in the nursery. I shed my bonnet and spencer and go into my parlor, closing the door behind me. Then I stand in the center of the room, watching without really seeing as dust motes dance in the sunlight that slants through the windows.

It is too quiet in here. I look down at the books I still carry and my entire body is at once consumed with agitation. I think of Mr. Travis's sudden discomfort—oh, I should have said something to put him at ease. My own station in life is not so very high, after all.

And yet—Mr. Travis has never left Kent.

My fingers open and close around the bindings, and then I turn away from the window and sit abruptly in my favorite chair. There is nothing pressing for me to attend to; I can read in peace awhile.

I look for a moment at Dr. Hill's *Herbal*, thinking, *He thought of me.* And then I shake my head, sending implications scattering, and set the book aside, covering it, after a moment's thought, with my whitework. I open my novel and scan the first line, and then the second. My toes move restlessly within my half boots; my gaze refuses to lie still upon the page but darts, without particular focus, about the room until it lands on the corner of the book poking out from under my embroidery. I drag it back, read another line. Close the book and sit with my lips pressed together.

There is a tentative knock at the parlor door, and I start. The novel slides to the floor as the door opens.

"There you are," William says, entering the room. "Did you have an enjoyable walk into town?"

I resist the urge to scoop up the novel. "Very nice," I say.

He wanders about the room looking at our possessions as if seeing them for the first time. With one fingertip, he swipes at the top of a little round table, then raises the finger as if to inspect its cleanliness. I gather from his lack of comment that either Martha or Mrs. Baxter has dusted recently.

"Did you meet anyone of note?"

"No," I say quickly. With one foot I slide the novel back under my chair. "No one."

He is moving restlessly from one spot to the next; he picks up the porcelain shepherdess from its place on the mantel, puts it down again, and then does the same with the little painted bowl Elizabeth sent me from London. I watch him and hold in a sigh. He is bored, or putting off writing his sermon, or both.

"I saw Miss de Bourgh riding out; I thought perhaps you might have met her on the road."

"No," I say, "I did not have the pleasure of seeing her."

"A shame." He looks around and appears to really see me for the first time. He frowns, just a little. "What are you doing in here, my dear?"

I suppose it must seem odd that I am sitting here with nothing to occupy myself. "I was—going to take up some work," I say. "But I was just resting for a moment."

He is all sympathy. "Yes, it is so hot—I do not remember the last year it was so hot, so early in the year."

"Indeed." I feel a little of the same thrill I experienced when Lady Catherine visited yesterday, but underneath it lies a touch of shame. I have never made a secret of my trips to the circulating library, but William rarely sits still long enough to take notice of what I am reading or working on. But I cannot pretend not to know that, although he has never read a novel himself, he is opposed to them as a general rule—particularly for women, whose natural delicacy, he says, makes them especially vulnerable to the frivolity and dissipation between the covers. I keep a book of sermons in the room as well, in case he ever wishes me to read aloud; his patience rarely extends beyond six lines or so, and thus he has never noticed that the volume never changes.

I imagine the novel beneath my chair is glowing like an ember.

William leaves the parlor at last, as I knew he must; there is little enough to occupy him here. When the sound of his footsteps in the hall has faded, I crouch down in an undignified way to pick the book up off the floor, then rise and take the *Herbal* from its hiding spot. Opening the front drawer of my worktable, where I keep odd bits of ribbon and lace for which I have not yet found a use, I tuck both books inside.

IT IS A few days after my encounter with Mr. Travis at the library, and I am in the nursery, surrounded by the wreckage of my morning's work. Martha sits in a chair by the window, squinting in the dim light as she mends a tear in William's waistcoat. She has said nothing all morning, even as she watched me waste sheet after sheet of paper, rending them in my frustration and tossing them away until the floor was strewn with half-formed sketches. Even Louisa has lost interest in the game of chasing the papers around the room. Rain streams down the windowpanes, and the sky is covered by one vast, dark cloud, which suits my mood perfectly.

The sketches I copy directly from *The British Herbal* are fair imitations of the originals, but anything I try to create from life seems, incongruously enough, to lack the spark of life entirely. I will never, I fear, be truly proficient as an artist. Louisa's bloodless image, crinkled and torn, looks up at me from every corner of the room.

"I quite like this one, ma'am."

I look at Martha; she has finished with the waistcoat

and folded it neatly, and now sits with one of my drawings smoothed out across her lap. A hand, far lumpier and less well proportioned than it is in life, but with faithfully drawn square, clipped fingernails and the suggestion of skin that is thickly callused. I start to blush, and wish fervently that I could stop.

ouisa is walking. Just nine months old, and she took her first steps unaided from Martha's arms to mine two days ago. Since then, she has grown in confidence—she careens fearlessly off walls and furniture, thumps to the floor, and gets up again without fuss. I wrote to my mother yesterday to tell her the news, and I can already imagine her pained reply—my youngest brother was an early walker, and I can still remember my mother's despair at the bruises he sustained and the mischief he got into. But I cannot regret my own daughter's stumbling independence any more than I can help admiring her bravery in venturing into a world that must seem so very large.

We are in the garden, and though I know if William comes upon us he will be full of admonishments about the browning effects of too much sunlight, I have no wish to retire to the shade. I lean back on my hands and remove my bonnet, feeling the sun warm my hair, and watch Louisa weave her unsteady way across the lawn, her arms thrown out to either side for balance and her round face open and guileless. It is impossible to imagine her as a woman grown, a woman with a husband and children of her own, with thoughts and desires far more complicated than those she has now.

She stumbles slightly but rights herself before she falls, and then looks back at me for praise. I clap my hands together.

How odd to think that someday her heart and mind will no longer be so open to me; they will fill with secret thoughts and wishes to which I will not be privy. I think of all the things I have kept from my mother over the years, large and small, and I ache.

From somewhere behind me, I can hear William humming to himself as he goes about his watering. His voice is surprisingly appealing, the air he hums light and cheerful, yet I can feel the muscles in my neck growing tense at the prospect of his coming closer. I bite my lip and look on as Louisa bends toward a stand of foxgloves and, before I can call out a reprimand, snatches one of the pale purple blossoms in her fist. I close my mouth as she toddles on, the flower clutched to her chest. William's humming seems louder, but I do not look around to see where he is.

One day, I think, Louisa will want to hear about her parents' romance. When we were young, both Maria and I asked our own mother countless times how she and our father met, fell in love, and decided to marry.

Each time, she told us patiently how they met when she came as a girl to visit her widowed aunt in Meryton. "We went into the shop for some yellow ribbon, and there your father stood, straight and tall and smiling, behind the counter. How handsome he was!"

"And you loved him at once?" Maria always said, and our mother smiled a little.

"He was so cheerful, so agreeable, how could I not admire him?" she said. "And my aunt did much to promote the match, for she loved me and wanted me near her always."

My mother's father, who operated a warehouse in London, was also eager for his daughter to live in the country, where the air seemed to agree with her much more than did the smoggy air in town.

"Your father called on me nearly every day for three weeks, after we were first introduced," our mother said.

"What did you talk about?" I asked, for in truth, it was rare to hear my parents converse about anything that did not pertain to the household.

"Oh—many things," my mother answered vaguely. "He was always so attentive and paid me the loveliest compliments. It came as no surprise when he finally proposed."

"And by *then*, you were very much in love," Maria said with happy conviction.

Once again, my mother smiled a little. "Indeed."

It never occurred to me, until just now, that when she answered, my mother might have been lying.

For what can I tell Louisa but a lie? The truth is not an option.

"Your papa was refused by Mrs. Darcy," I might say, were I being truthful. *"So I contrived to put myself in his path when his pride was hurt and he was especially vulnerable to flattery."*

Well, that will never do.

I FIRST MET William at a ball in Hertfordshire, where he was a guest of his cousins the Bennets. He was fully himself from the first moments of our acquaintance, simpering and strange, bowing over my hand in a manner that was almost servile. His behavior toward my friend Eliza was so marked that no one could have missed it, and her mortification was just as obvious—except, it seemed, to him. When they danced, she held herself with unusual stiffness, and he moved with no grace at all, his timing just off from the music. More than once, he turned in the wrong direction.

He asked me to dance later in the evening, and it was a trying experience; conversation was impossible, as he had to concentrate so fully on the steps.

He proposed to Eliza the very next morning, and though I had expected nothing else, I could not help but see her inevitable refusal as foolish. Lizzy is younger than I by seven years, and prettier by far, and she had romantic notions about marriage. But she had little in the way of a dowry, and now she was fortunate enough to be the object of a man's affection—a man who was, for all his many foibles, well situated in life, with a comfortable living in Kent and the promise of inheriting Longbourn upon Mr. Bennet's death. With the entail of her father's estate firmly settled upon Mr. Collins, nothing could make Elizabeth's mother and four unwed sisters safer than to keep the estate within the family.

I was ashamed of the envy that curled in my belly—envy that a man wanted her; envy that she was secure enough in her own mind and sure enough of her own prospects to reject him.

NOT LONG AFTER, the entire Longbourn party came to dine at Lucas Lodge. Elizabeth made a face at me, half-laughing, half-apologetic, from across the table, when Mr. Collins took the seat my mother indicated beside me—a look that Mr. Collins clearly caught, for I felt him grow very still at my side.

It was a rather dreadful dinner, really, for Mr. Collins's refused proposal hung heavily over the room, known by all but not openly acknowledged. My mother and Jane, the eldest of the Bennet girls, were occupied in trying to find neutral topics of conversation, while Mrs. Bennet interspersed too-quick, too-cheerful remarks with black looks in Elizabeth's direction. From the corner of my eye, I watched as Mr. Collins's long fingers opened and closed in spasms around his spoon.

I set my own spoon down and turned deliberately in his direction. Even by candlelight, I could see the red of mortification on his cheeks. "Do tell me, Mr. Collins," I said, "from where did you come before you found your place in Kent?"

He looked at me, clearly startled. "I am from Suffolk, Miss Lucas," he said.

I did my best to smile encouragingly. "I have never been there, but I have heard it is a beautiful county."

"Well," he said, "it is pretty enough, I daresay, though I must say I prefer my situation now." He leaned toward me and added with great seriousness, "Do you know that I can see the rooftop of Rosings Park from the windows of my humble abode?" When I shook my head, he said, "Oh, yes! And a very handsome rooftop it is—more than *thirty thousand* slate tiles! And not a one in need of repair, for Lady Catherine is *most* attentive to all the details of her estate's upkeep."

My voice caught at the back of my throat as I tried to reply, and I had to swallow. "That does sound . . . most agreeable," I said at last. "And how long have you been in Kent?"

From her seat opposite, Lizzy sent me a look of gratitude as he spoke—at length, and with much enthusiasm—about his life as the parson at Hunsford parish. He used his hands to great effect as his voice rose, gesticulating to emphasize a point and, once, nearly upsetting my wineglass in his fervor. I nodded and smiled in the proper places. Mr. Collins seemed to grow larger under my attention, swelling as his self-assurance returned until I felt almost crowded by the bulk of him in the chair beside me. His elbow jostled mine, and he then was most anxious to assure me he had not meant to take such a liberty.

I watched the changing expressions on his face as he spoke; I listened to the earnestness of his voice. He was not an attractive young man; he was heavy of cheek and jowl, with slightly irregular features and thinning hair, and his manners were so awkward that it was hard, at times, to keep my countenance as he veered from unaccountable pomposity to slavish compliments. The longer I spent in his company, the more impossible it became to imagine Elizabeth married to him; though she delights in small doses of the ridiculous, she has never been very tolerant of the faults of others.

As I sat there beside him, I began to feel rather as if I were outside myself. The sounds of the others at the table—their voices, the clink of silverware—receded, and I heard only Mr. Collins's stumbling voice. I was acutely aware of the details of him—the way he wet his lips with his tongue when he had been speaking for a long while; the large curling shells of his ears; the odd impression his neckcloth gave of trying to strangle him. He made a comment about the grand dining room at Rosings Park; I smiled, and his gratitude was such that a bright sureness bloomed within me.

I can have him, I thought with an odd detachment. It was not an idle hope; it was a certainty. *I* was capable of doing what Elizabeth was not. I could listen to this man without deriding him; I could endure his company and keep my composure. A little encouragement, a little attention—he needed these things, and if I gave them to him, I could have him, and all he had to offer, in return.

It is hard to think well of men when they so obviously do not think well of you. Though my head was turned once or twice when I was just a girl, as I never turned any heads myself, it became easy to observe the men of my acquaintance with a critical eye rather than a hopeful one. And what I saw did not impress, so that, except for the obvious brutes, one man began to seem much like another. Mr. Collins was ridiculous; but what was a bit of silliness compared to a lifetime of dependency?

During the main course, he broke off suddenly, noticing that my plate was still mostly full. "Miss Lucas," he said, and the redness returned to his cheeks in a great rush. "I am keeping you from your dinner . . ."

In the time since, I have looked back upon that moment, seeing it with such clarity that it is as if I am still there, seated beside William at my parents' table, poised on the precipice of an irrevocable choice. I teetered there, looking at his round, plain face, for a long moment. And then:

"Your conversation is such a pleasure, Mr. Collins, that I quite forgot to eat," I said. I lifted my glass and took a sip of wine but made no move toward my fork. "Pray, continue."

WILLIAM COMES AROUND the bend in the path. He is still humming to himself. His shirtsleeves are rolled up, showing forearms that are nearly hairless, and his hat is pushed back on his head so that his face is ruddy from the sun. In one hand is a small posy of early summer blooms that he must have just clipped. He looks as contented as I have ever seen him, and when he spies Louisa and me, he smiles.

Chapter Thirteen

My sister, Maria, is marrying for love.

The letter was waiting for me at the post office, along with another, written in an unfamiliar scrawl, for Mrs. Fitzgibbon from her own sister. I sit reading Maria's in a field just outside the village, Louisa crouched beside me. In one fist she holds the bread I brought with me to keep her satiated on our walk.

I have read the letter over twice, and still I cannot entirely believe its contents. When last Maria wrote, only a month past, she bemoaned Meryton's scarcity of eligible men. And now . . .

I should be filled with joy. I read her words yet again, look at Louisa, pick her up, and press her against my belly. She wriggles, the bread trapped between us.

"Shall we go visit our friend?" I say.

MRS. FITZGIBBON IS kneeling among her vegetables. Louisa squirms fiercely in my arms; I put her down and she stumble-runs across the field, her white bonnet, just a little too big, slipping down over one eye, the leading ribbons I sewed to the shoulders of her dress sailing behind her.

"Oh, my sweet lamb!" Mrs. Fitzgibbon cries, and holds her arms wide. Louisa rushes into her embrace. "Just look at you!" She leans her head back to look up at me. "Walking, the clever girl! When did this start?"

"Only days ago; she seems to have a particular talent for it." I reach into my reticule and hold out her letter. "I am sorry for the early hour, but this was waiting for you at the post office. I thought you would be eager to read it."

Mrs. Fitzgibbon stares at the letter as if she has never seen such a thing before. When she reaches for it, her hand trembles. "From Sarah," she says, so softly, running her thumb over the paper. With great economy, her sister has cross-written her letter in a very small, cramped hand, lines running from side to side as well as up and down the page. "Oh, Mrs. Collins—"

She gently moves Louisa aside and rises. Her joints creak. Then, "I'll just be a moment," and she vanishes into the cottage. When she reappears, she is dragging two chairs from her kitchen.

"Let's sit out here," she says. I take one of the chairs from her hastily. "It's so nice and cool."

The air still feels close and thick, but there is a blanket

of clouds spread across the sky; what little light that filters through is feeble. Without the sun's full weight, the day does feel almost cool.

Still . . . "Louisa and I should leave you to your letter, Mrs. Fitzgibbon. I know how much you have longed for word from your sister."

But Mrs. Fitzgibbon shakes her head. "It can wait. It will give me something to look forward to, and right now, I've the pleasure of your company." She ducks back into the cottage before I can respond and returns with something cupped in one hand.

"A sweetie," she says, and holds out her hand, palm up, to show me the lump of sugar. I nod, and her smile becomes a grin; she hands the sugar to Louisa, who takes it, sticks it in her mouth, and sucks.

"You will spoil her," I say, but I cannot help the way my mouth tugs up at the corners.

"Nonsense." Mrs. Fitzgibbon sits in the second chair and lets out a sigh. "Children need spoiling, and mine never lived long enough for me to spoil them. Though perhaps it was for the best, after all." She glances at me and lowers her voice, as if to keep Louisa from hearing. "Mr. Fitzgibbon liked his drink, and when he was in his cups he was a handy man with his fists. I don't know but that it would have broken my heart to have my children used as he used me."

I cannot imagine being treated so roughly that having

my children perish in infancy would be preferable to their enduring the same. I look at Louisa, sucking on her sugar lump, and I think of her brother, whose life I have always thought I would have given anything to extend, and shudder.

Mrs. Fitzgibbon seems to sense my mood. "Well, and it was long ago, now," she says. "In the end, he was too ill to work—not that he ever did much of that anyway—or even to drink." She watches my hand as it traces the edge of my letter.

"News from home?" she says leadingly.

I look at Louisa, who rocks back on her bottom as she enjoys her treat. "From my sister," I say. "She is engaged."

"Oh, how lovely." Mrs. Fitzgibbon tilts her head. "Is it not?"

I can feel the doubtful expression upon my face and struggle to smooth it out. "Of course it is. She is marrying for love."

The old woman settles back with a snort. "Well, I married for love," she says, and then looks sorry for the words. She glances sideways at me. "Good fortune to your sister," she adds, with a skeptical sort of sincerity.

"I HAVE SOME news."

William looks up from his plate. Dinner tonight is cottage pie, his favorite dish. Mrs. Baxter looked at me askance when I requested the change to the menu—"It is so hot, Mrs. Collins; are you sure you would not prefer something less rich?"—but I insisted.

"What is it, my dear?" he says.

"I have had a letter from Maria. She—she is engaged."

"Engaged!" William says, and actually sets down his fork. "What is the gentleman's name?"

"Mr. Cowper. George Cowper."

"I hope he is worthy of her?"

I know what William is not saying, and bite the inside of my cheek.

"He is an apothecary," I say at last.

"An—oh, my dear. That is not—her ladyship will not—" William brings his hands to his chest, pressing against the front of his waistcoat, his face full of dismay.

"The match may not be grand," I say quickly, "but Maria seems very happy. She writes that she hopes we will be able to attend the wedding."

William shakes his head slowly. "Lady Catherine may not be able to spare me."

This is nonsense. I toy with my fork. "They are to be married in September, just after the harvest," I say. "Maria understands that your duties must keep you in Kent until then, at least—"

"I am expected at the ball," William says. "Her ladyship depends upon me."

"I know that," I say evenly. The harvest ball at Rosings Park is always the event of the season in Hunsford. "That is why they are delaying the wedding until autumn. It is very important to Maria that I—that we—be there."

William's distress is still obvious, but he appears to be attempting to moderate it for my sake. He takes a bite of pie and chews loudly.

"Well," he says at last, tone doubtful, "it is not as though her intended is a common laborer, is it? It must be a relief to your parents to have her . . . settled."

It is as close to tactful as William is capable of being. Almost, I could love him for it.

THE DRAWING ROOM at Rosings is very dark, all the heavy curtains drawn. Miss de Bourgh must be suffering from one of her headaches. I am put in mind of Mrs. Fitzgibbon's shadowy cottage and wonder what she would think to see these great big windows, all covered up.

Miss de Bourgh reclines upon a chaise longue with a handkerchief covering her eyes. Mrs. Jenkinson sits beside her, her hands idle, for it is too dim for reading or sewing. I wonder, as William and I approach Lady Catherine and make our bows, how long she has been sitting so. Lady Catherine pulls her eyes away from her daughter to acknowledge our greetings, her mouth a puckered line.

We are here by her invitation, but the circumstances are hardly conducive to a lively visit. Almost, I offer apologies for disturbing them, but tuck my tongue against the roof of my mouth; presumably, Lady Catherine would have informed us had she wished to rescind the offer of tea. William sits very still beside me, fingers laced together in his lap and feet carefully still upon the floor. Silence descends, broken only by the maid's entering with tea and cake.

"Your husband informs me that your younger sister is engaged to be married." Lady Catherine's words are a hiss, almost too low for me to catch. She stirs sugar into her tea and looks at me expectantly. William's eyes dart between us.

"Yes, Your Ladyship," I say.

"It is a pity she did not make a better match. I cannot imagine what she was thinking of—what your father was thinking of to allow it. Miss Lucas struck me as a very sensible girl when she visited here." Lady Catherine takes a bite of cake, chews with soft smacks of her lips. I hold my peace; I know enough to know that she is not yet ready for my response.

"She is a gentlewoman," she says. "Even though your father has little in the way of property or fortune, she *is* a gentlewoman, and as such she has obligations to her family! Why, how will your brothers' marriages be affected by this alliance? How will your own daughter's?" She shakes her head. "Your poor mother—how I pity her."

I duck my head at the mention of Louisa; William's head bobs. "Mrs. Collins and I are unable to account for this, Your Ladyship, I assure you—"

"Lower your voice, if you please, Mr. Collins," Lady Catherine snaps, and William claps a palm to his mouth. Her ladyship's gaze slides toward Miss de Bourgh, who has not moved at all. After a little silence, she sighs and looks at me.

"Mr. Collins says you wish to attend the wedding."

I swallow. "I do, ma'am. Maria is my only sister; it would feel . . . wrong not to attend her wedding."

"Sentiment," Lady Catherine says with a sniff, and I cannot disagree.

Chapter Fourteen

I have not spoken to Mr. Travis since he left me with such haste outside the circulating library. After church on Sunday he chose not to linger with the other farmers, who gathered and talked in the cool shadows under the May tree at the edge of the green, but instead left after the service was concluded, and though I went once to visit his father, the son was toiling in a far field and, so far as I know, did not even know I was there, though my heart trip-trapped against my ribs when I spotted his figure in the distance.

Today, I am sitting with old Mr. Travis in his garden. The blanket we brought with us is spread upon the ground under me, soft and thick. Old Mr. Travis is dozing on his bench, an empty plate beside him with only a few soft, sweet crumbs remaining of his slice of the seed cake I baked this morning. Martha has Louisa by the leading ribbons, allowing the baby to explore the garden without letting her get close enough to harm the herbs and flowers.

"We heard a rumor," says a quiet, familiar voice from behind me, "that there was cake."

I look around at Mr. Travis. His dark hair is untidy and his clothes are dusty from the fields, but his hands, clasped together before him, have been scrubbed clean. There is uncertainty behind his eyes when they meet my own, and I feel annoyance rise—with him, for the gift of a borrowed book and for his sudden, strange vulnerability, and with myself, for accepting his offering and for the way I seem always to respond to his presence in such a nonsensical way. He is neither especially handsome nor especially learned, at least not in the things that matter in polite society; and yet I feel pulled to him, as if I am wearing invisible ribbons at the shoulders of my dress and he holds the other ends.

But I have never made a fool of myself over a man, and I refuse to start doing so now. "There is cake," I say lightly, and cut a slice for him and one for Henry Peters, his young farmhand, who hovers at Mr. Travis's side as if uncertain he belongs here. They eat, Henry very quickly and with mumbled thanks before he returns to his work. But Mr. Travis remains; his eyes follow Martha and Louisa as they take their turns around the garden, and at last he looks to me, delight in the lines about his mouth.

"This is new," he says.

"Louisa is very proud of herself. And your father was in raptures when she came to him on her own, with no hand to steady her."

"As he should have been. It is a great accomplishment. The first of many, I'm sure."

My laugh comes out as a gust of warm air. "I hope she is more accomplished than her mother, at least."

He looks at me inquiringly; I recline upon my forearms and stare at Louisa. Her bonnet is askew; her entire body is given over to the delight of her own physicality and to the thrill of exploration. Her two teeth stand out tipsily in her open, laughing mouth.

"I have no accomplishments," I say at last.

"I find that difficult to believe."

"Why? Because I am the daughter of a gentleman?"

Mr. Travis comes nearer. "May I?" he says, indicating the blanket, then settles himself upon it at my nod. He cants his head upward to look at the sky; my eyes are drawn to the sharp protrusion of his Adam's apple and the faint shadow of bristles over his cheeks and throat.

"Because you told me yourself that you once loved to draw," he says. "And—yes—forgive me, but I suppose I have always been under the impression that gently bred ladies have little to do *but* collect accomplishments."

"Your impression was mistaken, at least in my case. Some gentlemen's daughters spend a good portion of their day in the kitchen."

He looks at me. I press my lips together and raise my brows. "*I* made the cake I brought today," I say in response to his unspoken question. "My family has no cook, and so my mother and sister and I prepared all of our meals. My father was a merchant, Mr. Travis, until I was nearly a woman grown. When he—decided—to buy a small estate and sell his business it was . . . not the soundest of decisions." I think of my mother's dismay, of coming upon her once as she cried helplessly in the larder after my father announced his decision. *We will all starve*, she said, and though it was never anywhere near so dire as that, we did have to economize. We had a maid but no cook; we made over our dresses, sometimes more than once, rather than buy new ones.

"I had no drawing master and no governess," I say. "Any—little—ability I have is entirely self-gleaned. What I do would certainly not be recognized as *accomplished* by anyone in Lady Catherine's sphere."

But now I think of Mrs. Fitzgibbon's mean little cottage, so dark even during the day, with only the one room in which to cook and eat and receive visitors; of her single delicate porcelain cup, so obviously cherished. Of the fact that she had not corresponded with her sister in years, for want of just a little extra money. Everything I imagine I lack seems petty in the face of true deprivation.

"You must think me . . . quite ridiculous," I say.

"No." A pause, and a sly smile. "*No* accomplishments at all?"

I laugh—too high, too shrill, and I glance quickly at the elder Mr. Travis to make sure I have not woken him. "None," I say. "That is—I can draw, a very little. And play—a very, *very* little. My mother was in charge of my education, and she cannot paint, she speaks no other languages . . . She did make sure we could dance, for how else were we to meet men?" My smile is thin. "Louisa will be better educated than I was, at least. I will make sure of that."

"Mrs. Collins," Mr. Travis says slowly, "I owe you an apology."

I say, "Oh, no—" with reflexive politeness.

He shakes his head. "I was discourteous when last we met. I have no excuse—"

"It's forgotten," I say quickly, and he subsides, but I can feel him watching me. I think, as I have so often since it arrived, of Maria's letter. I wonder what she and her Mr. Cowper talk about.

"My sister is engaged," I say.

"That is excellent news."

"It is." Of course it is. It *is*. "She seems very happy."

His eyes remain steadily upon my face. "That is as it should be when one is engaged, is it not?"

"Yes," I say. In fact, *happy* does not do justice to Maria's effusions—there is no man more handsome or with a more engaging manner; her Mr. Cowper carries himself well and dances beautifully. He is witty and kind, and everything about him is so very agreeable that she cannot imagine they will ever argue. I clear my throat, avert my eyes. I cannot bear the pressure of his scrutiny. "They have not been acquainted for very long. That is—why this is a surprise."

"Ah." He looks out over the garden for a moment, then adds in a careful way, "Of course, it does not follow that a short acquaintance means the match will be unhappy."

"Of course not." I pause. "Mr. Collins and I became engaged after only truly conversing twice." I flick a glance at him and then away.

"*Ah*," he says again.

"Lady Catherine and Mr. Collins are both disappointed by the match."

I want to stuff my fist into my mouth, stopper myself like a bottle. I must find a way to keep my every thought from spilling from my throat when I am around this man. His mere presence cuts through the heavy layers of my reserve as if they are so much net.

"Why is that?"

I touch my lips together, then say, "Because—Maria's intended—he is an apothecary."

A raised brow. "A worthy profession."

"Yes. But—it is a *profession*."

Mr. Travis snorts quietly. "And there's the rub," he murmurs. I stare, wrong-footed by his use of such a reference; he looks back without expression.

"Really, it is not such an unequal match," I say. "It would have been perfectly eligible if my father had not been knighted. We are not—Maria does not even have a dowry."

His laugh has a sharp edge. "But he *was* knighted."

"She sounds so happy," I say once more.

The compassion in his eyes is suddenly intolerable, and I look down.

Louisa chooses now to crumple to the ground with a petulant cry, suddenly overcome by tiredness after so much exertion. As we both watch, she lashes out at the surrounding grass with fists and fingers.

"Oh, love," I say on a breath, and hold out my arms. Martha brings her to me and settles her in my lap, where she rubs her knuckles against her eyes and whines as I rock her gently, back and forth.

Mr. Travis plucks long strands of grass and begins to weave them together, his big fingers managing the delicate work with incongruous ease. When he is finished, he holds out the grass plait.

"For you, little miss," he says, startling Louisa out of her ill temper. After a moment she takes it in her fist, examining it; then she waves it madly. He grins.

Chapter Fifteen

I am weeding the kitchen garden when Mrs. Baxter pokes her head through the doorway. "Mrs. Collins," she says, "Mr. Collins asks that you join him in the front parlor."

I raise an eyebrow, spread my hands to show their dirtiness. "Tell Mr. Collins I will be in in a moment."

She shakes her head. "It's urgent, ma'am. Her ladyship has come to call."

Oh, bother. I stand and rub my hands vigorously with the hem of my apron, then untie the apron and give it over to Mrs. Baxter. "Thank you," I say even as I hurry through the kitchen and into the house proper, tucking flyaway strands of hair under my cap and smoothing down my dress as I go. When I open the parlor door, William half-stands.

"Charlotte, my dear," he says. "Lady Catherine was just telling me that she has some news!"

I make my curtsy, which Lady Catherine receives with a slight inclination of her head, and take my seat on the chair beside William. "Indeed, ma'am?"

William leans forward, palms against his thighs. "I was just saying to Lady Catherine that it must be news of great import, for her to condescend to call upon *us* to discuss it!" He looks at me pointedly.

"Yes," I say. "We are all eagerness."

Her ladyship smiles, just a little. "I have received a letter from my nephew Mr. Darcy." She pauses dramatically. "He wrote to say that he and his family will be visiting Rosings in just a few weeks. They will be here in time for the harvest ball."

William clasps his hands together, and I only just prevent myself from doing the same. Eliza! Here! Lady Catherine's eyes slide to me, and her satisfied smile drops away.

"No doubt you will receive a letter of your own informing you of this news, Mrs. Collins."

I make my tone as conciliatory as I can. "Yes, probably, Your Ladyship."

"It is no more than the duty and honor that he owes to me and Anne," she says at length. "But—aside from his unfortunate marriage—Darcy has always been very attentive to duty. And he has told me," she says, a little of her satisfaction returning, "that Mrs. Darcy has taken my advice about the new chair covers for the music room at Pemberley."

LADY CATHERINE DEPARTS and I return to the garden. I am joyful at the prospect of seeing Elizabeth again; I sing as I pluck weeds from among the vegetables. My voice is thin, and I would never dream of performing among company, but just now, with the sun pressing warm against my back, the smell of the earth in my nose, and the thought that soon my friend will be here, I cannot help myself.

"DO YOU THINK that my cousin and her husband will honor us with a visit during their stay at Rosings Park?"

I look up from the shift I am sewing. William stands in the doorway to my parlor. He is so large, and my parlor is so small, that his presence feels all the more intrusive. I stab my needle into the cloth and set it aside.

"I certainly hope so," I say, "unless Lady Catherine requires their attendance constantly."

"You must prepare the house just as if they were coming to stay with us," he says, looking around. "My cousin is, of course, used to much grander accommodations than when last she came into Kent, but it would not do for her or Mr. Darcy to find fault with our home, however humble it may be."

"I had not planned for there to be reason for them to find

fault," I say, with more asperity than I usually allow when speaking to William. But he seems not to notice.

"Perhaps you might ask her ladyship if she can suggest any improvements before Mr. and Mrs. Darcy arrive."

My eyes close, just briefly. "Of course." Almost, I say that perhaps he might ask Lady Catherine for advice about his gardens; but it is more likely that he would miss the slight and take the advice seriously. And what if Lady Catherine were to suggest some improvement that required Mr. Travis's help? I pick up the shift again, keeping my eyes on my stitches so I do not have to look at my husband. My husband, who does not deserve my cruelty, even in thought.

He sits heavily in the chair across from mine. I make a stitch, and then another. He will leave soon, no doubt; he hasn't the temperament for sitting still.

He lets out a great sigh, and I lower the shift. Though conversation is not our strength, perhaps a little of it might speed him on his way. "What is it?" I say; I am pleased that my voice does not betray my irritation. "You seem troubled."

William rests his elbows on the arms of his chair and holds his hands up before his face, fingertip to fingertip.

"I am glad they come for the ball," he says.

I look down at my lap. At the ball, Elizabeth and her husband will see William presiding over the proceedings alongside her ladyship. They will see his importance here. Neither of us has ever acknowledged that before he proposed to me,

William requested Lizzy's hand in marriage; but I remember the way we both fretted about every detail before she, my father, and Maria came to visit after we were wed. I am less anxious now, but William, it seems, is not.

"Elizabeth has always loved a dance," I say for want of something better.

He clears his throat. "Yes. I remember. She was always . . . too lively, really."

I glance at him, and his eyes widen.

I have only a moment to wonder what it is he imagines he sees in my face, and then suddenly he is out of his chair and kneeling beside my own; I nearly stick him with the needle in my surprise. "My dearest Charlotte," he says, and clasps my free hand in both his own. "I hope you do not think— you mustn't distress yourself—Lady Catherine was most eloquent on the subject of my cousins' misfortune—it seemed that an easy means of alleviating their distress was in my power—but I would not for the world have you think—" He presses my hand between his palms, apparently overcome; I can only look on in amazement.

"God and Lady Catherine sent me to Hertfordshire," he says. "And I know that it was so that *we,* my dear, who are the most perfectly suited of all couples, might find each other." He raises my hand to his lips.

I do not know what to say, and so I am silent. William cradles my hand in his own; I want to pull away. And then, all at once, I think of Mrs. Fitzgibbon's brute of a husband, and I am lanced with a fierce gratitude for William's gentle foolishness. For his own part, William seems content to smile up at me from his awkward position. The clock strikes the hour, and he glances from it to my face. "Do you mean to work much longer, my dear?"

He can mean only one thing by that question, and after such a declaration as he just made, I can do nothing but set my sewing aside. "No," I say. "I suppose not."

HE FALLS ASLEEP immediately after, and I am left awake beside him, my mind unquiet. I drum my fingers against my thighs, flex and release my toes. William snorts in his sleep, and I roll over on my side so that I am facing the breadth of his back. It moves gently as he breathes. I put out a hand but do not quite touch him.

It is strange to think that I know this man so intimately, and, at the same time, so little. I know his habits as if they were my own. His tastes, his peculiarities, the way he smells, the weight of his body on top of mine. But there is something, some essential thing, missing—there must be more to him than these accumulated details.

I think of his lips on my hand, the fervency of his assurances in the parlor. My fingers curl back into my palm and I draw my hand away from his back. Sometimes I have moments of pure astonishment when I realize that William, it seems, is very sure that he knows all of me. He believes that I am the person he sits across from at dinner every evening; he thinks he understands the woman with whom he lies at night. I suppose this means that I am a good wife. But I cannot think of a single time that I have shared more than the barest surface of my thoughts with him, and keeping myself always in check can sometimes feel so very draining.

I roll over and put my fingers to my lips, close my eyes.

Perhaps, I think, just as I begin to relax into sleep, William does not give himself fully to me, either. The thought seems unlikely, absurd, but it is disconcerting, nevertheless, and my eyes open again. Perhaps we are both caught in this elaborate pantomime.

Chapter Sixteen

There is a thrumming throughout the congregation today—I can feel it under my boots, in the vibrations in the air around me. I keep my eyes upon William, who reads his sermon placidly without seeming aware of the charge to the atmosphere, his emphases, as usual, in entirely odd places; but I am distracted.

After the service, Mr. Travis greets both William and myself as he leaves the church. "A moment," I say, and draw him a little aside with the excuse of asking after his father.

"He is well, thank you," Mr. Travis says. He looks down at me, the lines about his eyes deepening as he smiles.

We speak of the harvest, which is nearing, and the preparations at Rosings Park for the harvest ball, with which William has lately been very preoccupied. "Will your father attend, do you think?" I ask. The Meryton assemblies were always filled with men and women whose dancing days were long behind them but who seemed still to find enjoyment in the close company of so many people.

Mr. Travis shakes his head. "I will be surprised if he does, though I've no doubt he will encourage me to attend regardless. He is . . . he moves so slowly, these days. I do not know that he could manage the walk to Rosings Park."

"I wish we kept a carriage, so that I might offer it to you and your father from time to time."

"I doubt if he would accept. He is . . . maddeningly prideful at times. And the older he gets, the more stubborn he becomes."

Speaking of the ball makes me think of Elizabeth, and I am suddenly refilled with some of yesterday's exuberance. "I have news," I say, the words bursting forth, and oh, it feels good to share my joy. "My dear friend Mrs. Darcy is coming here in time for the ball."

"This must make you very happy," he says, with such warmth that I feel, with sudden certainty, that my happiness is of special interest to him, and I am all at once disconcerted. I struggle to take up the conversation again.

"I—yes, it does. Make me happy, that is. To see my friend, and then so soon after to see my family—for Lady Catherine has given leave for us to visit Hertfordshire for my sister's wedding—yes. I am very happy."

"I am glad."

My cheeks are too warm, and I cannot think what to say next. But Mr. Travis replaces his hat and says, "I fear my father will be expecting me. Have a good day, Mrs. Collins."

"Oh—of course." I nod as he bows. "Good day." A quick smile, a lingering glance, and he is gone, pausing only briefly to exchange greetings with another farmer.

I turn away, force myself to think of what I should be doing. I ought to collect Louisa so Martha can go home with her family, and so the baby can nap—

"Mrs. Collins! Oh, Mrs. Collins!"

It is Mrs. Prewitt, the draper's wife, bearing down upon me like a great ship, the ribbons on her bonnet trailing behind her like sails. She has the arm of a young woman I have never seen before threaded through her own. "Mrs. Collins!" she says again, puffing slightly, when they have reached me. "I am glad we did not miss you—may I present my niece, Miss Mary Harmon? Mary, this is Mrs. Collins."

Miss Harmon makes a pretty little curtsy. She is, I think, somewhere between twenty and five-and-twenty, with smooth pale hair and a pleasing figure. It is suddenly obvious what all the low, gossiping murmurs were about during the service; it is rare for a young woman of marriageable age to turn up in Hunsford.

"It is a pleasure to meet you, Miss Harmon," I say; she

smiles and murmurs a thank-you. Mrs. Prewitt, whose tongue is rarely still, hastens to fill the brief silence that follows.

"Mary is visiting from the north. My sister and her husband settled there some years ago—a beautiful place, but with such *nasty* weather!—and in all the time since her birth, Mary has never come here for a visit!"

"How do you find Kent?" I say.

Another smile. "It is lovely, Mrs. Collins. Though the journey here was a long one."

I open my mouth to respond, but Mrs. Prewitt is already talking.

"Oh, Mary adores Hunsford, don't you, Mary? In fact"— she lowers her voice in a conspiratorial fashion—"I've high hopes that she might settle here for good. It is hard to believe that a young woman so pretty and hardworking has not found a husband, but perhaps it is just as well, for she could have her pick among the bachelors here, I'm sure."

Miss Harmon colors. "Aunt," she says, and Mrs. Prewitt waggles a playful finger.

"Hush, my dear. There is no point in being missish about such things." She returns her attention to me. "Is there, Mrs. Collins? We all know how hard it is to catch a husband."

I force a smile.

"There are not," Mrs. Prewitt says, "*so* many eligible men in the village, but I can think of several possibilities. I shall count upon you, Mrs. Collins, to help me play matchmaker, for if you had not snapped up our parson, I daresay he would be top of my list!" She chortles while Miss Harmon and I glance at one another, and then, just as quickly, away.

I try to infuse my voice with the sort of laughing warmth at which Elizabeth has always excelled, but I fear I am falling short of the mark. "I will—ah—try to do my duty."

Mrs. Prewitt smiles widely and makes a show of glancing around at the villagers standing nearby, talking together in pairs and groups. More than one glance is cast our way, and I can see Miss Harmon's discomfort; obviously, she knows that she is the reason for so much attention. "Perhaps Mr. Ford," her aunt says. "He is perhaps a little gray, but Mary's father owns a delightful little inn—very respectable, or so Mr. Prewitt assures me—so it would be nothing for her to take up the work of a public house. Or perhaps a farmer—there is more than one I can think of who is in need of a wife. Mr. Green, or Mr. Travis." A sly glance at me. "*You* seem on quite friendly terms with Mr. Travis, Mrs. Collins! Perhaps you could put in a good word for Mary, here, when next you two have one of your little chats?"

I stare at her without sensation. "His father is not well," I say around a tongue that is suddenly desiccated. "I have been—that is—"

"Oh yes, his poor father," Mrs. Prewitt says. "But in any

case, it is just as well for *me* that you and Mr. Travis are friendly, as I said." And she winks at me.

There is a burning, a scraping, against my skin. I am certain, all at once, that the eyes upon us, the whispers, have little to do with Miss Harmon's arrival, after all.

Chapter Seventeen

William's shout is loud enough that I hear it, just faintly, even in the stillroom. Only a moment later, and he bursts through the doorway to find me with my arms poised above my head as I reach to fasten a bunch of rosemary to its hook for drying.

"They are here!" William says. "My dear—the Darcys have arrived at Rosings Park! I only just saw them pass."

I lower my hands, brush my fingers against the fabric of my apron. "They are earlier than I expected."

"No wonder—their horses are very fine beasts, and their carriage, Charlotte—such luxury! Their coachman wears the most elegant livery." He looks at the table, strewn with herbs I have yet to bundle and hang, and his brow creases anxiously. "This must be tidied."

"I will be finished shortly," I say, "though I do not think we can expect them *here* very soon, and even then, I hardly think Mr. and Mrs. Darcy are going to want to see our stillroom."

He chuckles, a nervous sound. "I suppose you are right, my dear. But still—just to be sure—"

"I will see to it," I say as soothingly as I can.

He returns to his book room, no doubt to resume watching the lane. For three days now, he has been watching the lane even more avidly than is usual for him, despite knowing that the Darcys were unlikely to arrive before today or tomorrow. Mrs. Baxter and Martha have been in a frenzy of cleaning and laundering. The parsonage looks as fine as ever it has.

I tie the last of the herbs into bunches and string them up, my fingers moving with the ease of practice while my mind drifts to thoughts of Rosings and what might be happening there. It is hard to imagine Elizabeth spending so much time in Lady Catherine's company; when she came to Kent after my marriage, she was by turns bored and amused by our audiences with her ladyship, though she was far too polite for her thoughts to be obvious to anyone who did not know her well. And she has not been back since, despite having married Lady Catherine's nephew. I try and fail to imagine my friend as a married woman, with a cap covering her dark hair and an attitude of deference toward her husband.

THE LETTER FROM Lizzy bearing the news of her engagement had come as such a shock that I found myself still sitting with it an hour later, mouth round with astonishment, when William arrived home from Rosings Park. He was gasping with the news that Lady Catherine had had a letter from her nephew Mr. Darcy, which contained the same information as the correspondence I still held in my hand, and that her ladyship was in a high fury.

"She has cut him off!" William said. "Entirely! She will never speak to him again. For him to have chosen someone like Cousin Elizabeth over Miss de Bourgh—it is unthinkable—so many hopes dashed." He managed to appear both aghast that his cousin had the temerity to go so expressly against Lady Catherine's wishes and thrilled that she had risen so high, for, "Now," he said, in a hushed tone, "I will be related to her ladyship by marriage."

WE ARE TO dine at Rosings. The invitation arrived not an hour after William left me in the stillroom; he has been alight with excitement all afternoon, banging around the house and driving me and Mrs. Baxter to distraction. Before we leave to walk across the lane and up the long drive to the house, I kiss Louisa good night, brushing my hand over her sleeping head. My fingers still smell of rosemary.

A footman shows us into the drawing room. Lady Catherine is seated in her usual place, with Miss de Bourgh and Mrs. Jenkinson beside her, and there, on the settee where William and I often sit, are Mr. Darcy and Elizabeth.

She smiles at me—a full smile, showing her teeth—but is otherwise restrained as we all make our greetings and William and I sit in the chairs Lady Catherine indicates. I look at Elizabeth, and she gives me that old, wry glance, just for a moment; and then Lady Catherine begins to speak, and Lizzy turns her attention to her.

"My nephew tells me that the roads were very dry all the way from Derbyshire," Lady Catherine says.

Mr. Darcy makes no effort to reply, and Elizabeth leans forward a little on her seat. "We could not have asked for better weather in which to travel. Truly, the journey was much easier than I expected, even with an infant."

I open my mouth to inquire after her son, but William is already talking.

"I happened to notice your carriage when you passed the parsonage, Mr. Darcy," he says. "If I may be so bold, I have rarely seen a handsomer equipage—excepting, of course, Your Ladyship's." He gives a nod to Lady Catherine that is more like a bow.

Mr. Darcy says, "Thank you, sir," and sets his jaw.

There is a little silence. Miss de Bourgh is looking off into the distance. I have long wondered whether she used to entertain the same hopes as her mother regarding marriage to her cousin, and looking at her now I cannot tell whether the disinterest she displays is genuine or affected. Her fingers toy with the fine embroidery at the edge of her shawl. I look at

Lizzy to find that she is watching Miss de Bourgh as well, a considering expression on her face—a face, I realize, that is a little rounder than it used to be. Elizabeth is altogether more plump than she once was, and it suits her, just as the gown she wears—made of a deep blue silk, with the most exquisite lace at the bodice—suits her, and the delicate jewels at her ears and throat. In contrast, her hair is arranged simply— very like she wore it in Hertfordshire—but there is no denying that her position has changed.

"You did bring him then?" I say, to break the silence. "Little Thomas?"

Lizzy smiles. "We did. He is with his nurse just now, but I would love to bring him to visit you tomorrow. And I must meet your daughter, of course—how old is she? She must be nearly a year."

"She is. She is walking, and she makes sounds that are *nearly* words—"

"I hope that you will play for us after dinner, Mrs. Darcy," Lady Catherine interrupts. Both Elizabeth and I subside, and William gives me a look of admonishment. "I understand from Georgiana's letters that you are learning from the same music master who taught her. I hope you have been practicing as diligently as my niece."

"I practice often, Lady Catherine," Elizabeth says. "Though my duties to Pemberley and to my family do take up a great deal of time."

"There is no excuse for—" But Lady Catherine breaks off, for the drawing room door has opened to admit a liveried footman.

"Dinner is served, ma'am," he says.

"I THOUGHT MY cousin looked very well," William says as we ready ourselves for bed. "Marriage and motherhood are good for her; she was far more restrained in her opinions than she used to be."

"Mmm." I remove the pins from my hair one by one and take up my hairbrush. From behind me comes the rustle of cloth as William removes his clothing.

"Mr. Darcy must be very pleased to return to Rosings," he says, his voice muffled as he pulls his nightshirt over his head. "I can only imagine the distress of being denied entry here for so long. Did you think he seemed pleased, my dear?"

Mr. Darcy was as taciturn tonight as I remember his being both in Hertfordshire and when he came to Kent just after my marriage. He was quiet at their wedding as well, though Mrs. Bennet was so talkative that she scarcely left room for anyone else to speak. Lizzy told me, when she wrote of her engagement, that Mr. Darcy's behavior had undertaken a dramatic change for the better, but this evening I could not see it.

I draw the brush through my hair again and again. "I imagine he is happy," I say.

"Yes." William sits on the edge of the bed. "How could he be otherwise?"

Lady Catherine's determination to never see her nephew again softened when she learned that Lizzy was with child—for, as she said to me over tea one day, Mrs. Darcy would need her guidance if she was to properly raise the heir to the Pemberley estate. Lizzy confessed to me in a letter that neither she nor Mr. Darcy could decide whether Lady Catherine's forgiveness was more blessing or curse.

"Make sure that Mrs. Baxter knows she must serve cake when they come to call tomorrow," William says as we settle into bed.

THERE IS PLUM cake, and the silver with which to eat it gleams from Mrs. Baxter's careful polishing. And there is plentiful sunshine, making the front parlor bright and cheerful. Were it not for the stream of nonsense issuing from William's mouth, I would be perfectly content. As it is, Lizzy and I have not managed to say more than three words to one another, and Mr. Darcy, who is the object of my husband's unwavering attention, seems to be making an effort to say as little as possible. Only baby Thomas seems unconcerned by the awkwardness in the room; he sits in his mother's lap, round faced and handsome, looking about him curiously.

"Mr. Collins," Mr. Darcy says suddenly, in the brief space between one of William's thoughts and the next; his voice is too forceful, and we all give little starts, William especially. "I hoped you might indulge me. I have the responsibility of installing a new rector at Lambton, and if it is agreeable to you I thought we might discuss the candidates. Your, er, expertise would be appreciated. Perhaps the ladies could enjoy a turn or two in your garden."

William touches the fingers of both hands to his lips and closes his eyes. "It would be my honor," he says after a moment, then stands quickly. "Mrs. Collins—be sure to show the roses to Mrs. Darcy. They were"—he gives a slight bow in Mr. Darcy's direction—"your aunt's idea entirely, Mr. Darcy, and let me assure you that her generosity and solicitude are felt deeply by both Mrs. Collins and myself. Come—we can adjourn to my book room; it is from the window there that I was fortunate enough to see your carriage pass yesterday morning . . ."

His voice fades as he goes down the hall. Mr. Darcy pauses to cast a look at Elizabeth that is at once exasperated and laughing, which she returns with a brilliant smile, and then he follows William from the room.

We hear the door to the book room close a moment later, and our eyes meet. Eliza's mouth twitches. "He knew I wanted time to visit alone with you," she says.

I should not laugh, not when William is, however obliquely, the butt of the joke, but I cannot help it. "How very inventive of him."

She steps toward me, and suddenly she has wrapped the arm not holding Thomas around me in a quick, fierce embrace. "I've missed you," she says.

WE HAVE BEEN nearly an hour in the garden together when we see Mr. Darcy and William emerge from the house, the latter looking much more pleased with the world than the former. Mr. Darcy comes straight to Elizabeth, who is sitting beside me on a bench with the baby in her arms. I collected Louisa from the nursery before coming outside, and she is exploring the nearby hedgerows, Martha following at a little distance.

"We should be going," Mr. Darcy says upon reaching us. "Lady Catherine will be expecting us for tea."

"And I am meant to practice the pianoforte for at least an hour before dinner." Lizzy's smile has a sardonic edge. "As you heard yourselves last night, my playing has not sufficiently improved for her ladyship's taste."

Lady Catherine winced and tutted through last night's performance, and dismissed Lizzy from the pianoforte when she had finished playing with a disgruntled wave of her hand.

"It would behoove you, my dear cousin, to take her ladyship's advice to heart," William says. "She wants only that the mistress of Pemberley be worthy of the role."

Mr. Darcy's face is a picture of outrage, but Elizabeth merely rises from the bench, obviously diverted.

"You are quite right, Mr. Collins, I am sure," she says. She turns to me. "I wish we could stay longer—"

I shake my head. "I understand. And we will see you at the ball in only a few days."

"If Lady Catherine does not invite you to tea or dinner before then." Elizabeth smiles, glancing at Mr. Darcy. "Now the families of Rosings and Pemberley are reconciled, I expect we will be visiting here more often—and hopefully for longer than a week next time."

Mr. Darcy makes a noncommittal noise, but the harsh lines of his face soften, just a little, when he looks at her.

William and I walk them to the gate, William pausing beside the rosebushes. I feel a little drop in the vicinity of my stomach and bend to neaten Louisa's bonnet, affecting deafness. But he only says, arms wide and palms raised, "These, Mr. Darcy, are the roses your aunt so magnanimously gifted us."

Lizzy and Mr. Darcy look. Even the single blossom has long since died, leaving the bushes looking more bedraggled than ever.

"They are," William hastens to add, "still immature, of course, and I could never presume to think that my garden could ever be the equal of Rosings's—or, indeed, of Pemberley's, Mr. Darcy, for I assure you that Lady Catherine speaks of your estate in the most flattering terms. But I do look forward to our roses reaching their potential—they can but stand as testimony to her ladyship's generous spirit."

After a pause, he adds, "They *are* rather small, still. Perhaps we ought to have Mr. Travis back to look at them."

I stand quickly, deafness forgotten. "No!" I say, with such vehemence that three pairs of startled eyes turn to stare at me. William's mouth gapes.

I inhale a steadying breath, take in the summer smells of sun and flowers. "My dear," I say, and my voice is calmer. "There is no need to bother Mr. Travis, not so close to the harvest. Perhaps after the ball, if you really think it necessary."

Elizabeth meets my eyes, one brow just slightly raised, as William makes a tetchy noise at the back of his throat.

I RETURN TO the lawn with Louisa and Martha and settle back on the bench while the two of them play at hide-and-seek among the hedgerows. I should really find something productive to do, but my body is listless, my mind pensive. My thoughts keep returning to Elizabeth and her husband and then shying away again. I feel almost embarrassed to have witnessed the affection that does, apparently, exist between them; and more than affection, a true intimacy of the sort Elizabeth always said she *must* have or never marry, the sort of intimacy that allows for communication without speech. I only saw a little—just moments, out of months and months of a marriage—but I am unsettled, as if I went for a walk in Rosings's woods and came across some lovely, fabled creature, the sort of thing one might tell children about in stories but which one never expects to find in life.

Unaccountably, there is the tingling behind my eyes that presages a hard, cleansing cry. I tip my head up and widen my eyes to keep the tears away. I want to ask Elizabeth so many impertinent questions, but I do not want to hear the inevitable sympathy in her response. Lizzy, pretty Lizzy, who refused the man whose later proposal to me was not repugnant, as it was to her, but salvation. Or so it seemed at the time.

Were I born with Elizabeth's looks, perhaps I'd have had other suitors at a much earlier age, though it is hard to imagine myself, under any circumstances, being a true romantic. Years of observing my parents' marriage, and the marriages of other couples in the neighborhood, had convinced me that wives guided their husbands subtly when they could and obeyed them when they must, and that felicity was something a woman found in other areas of her life—her children, perhaps, or her friends. My thoughts turn, as they so often have of late, to Mr. Travis. The book he borrowed was tangible proof that I am, at least sometimes, in his thoughts, that this improbable fixation is not entirely one-sided. The need to take to the woods seizes me, and I curl my fingers around the edge of the bench's seat to keep myself in place.

This would be no decorous stroll—if I let myself move, I

will run, and run, and run until my poor body cries out at me to stop. I will kick up dust from the lane, my gown will be hopelessly dirty; I will run like Louisa, heedless of how I look, until my bonnet flies off and bounces against my back, its ribbons catching around my throat.

I lean forward on the bench, rocking slightly with my hands still firmly anchoring me in my seat, and close my eyes. A deep inhale, the smell of the garden, the drone of the bees, and then Louisa's high laugh. My eyes open, catch and hold on the sight of my daughter—she stands, bonnet in hand, as Martha scolds her for removing it. Louisa's hair, so fine that pink scalp is visible, stands up all over her head in mad wisps, like seedlings just sprouting. When she laughs again, suddenly and for a reason that is obvious only to herself, her smile, with its uneven distribution of teeth, steals my breath entirely.

"Make her beautiful," I whisper, and it is not a prayer. It is an order, fierce and emphatic. My body hums with the force of it. I imagine my mother whispering those same words above my cradle; feel her creeping despair as it became clear, as the years passed, that her demand had not been answered. I carry her fear inside me now; it is a thread that connects us intimately, generation to generation. Louisa will never understand how desperately I love her, unless she has a daughter of her own.

Of course, when William inherits Longbourn Louisa will

have more prospects than I did. I have no doubt I will be able to ensure that William manages the estate more carefully than Mr. Bennet has, and so she will have a fine dowry. But still I long for the world to see her as I see her. The world *must* see her and recognize her worth. For I am not, for all the subjectivity of mother love, actually blind; though Louisa is still so small that it is hard to know how her features will change as she grows, I know the unlikelihood that William and I could ever create anything but a plain daughter. And yet—oh, no matter her looks, she is lovely, so lovely I ache with it. My girl turns in an unsteady circle, evading Martha's grasp, searching until she finds me with her eyes. She waves her bonnet like a flag of triumph. My heart beats hard and steady in time with the refrain inside my head.

Make her beautiful, make her beautiful, make her beautiful.

Chapter Eighteen

The harvest ball has been a tradition at Rosings Park since at least the time of Sir Lewis de Bourgh's father. William has been at Rosings every day helping with the preparations, though I have been unable to determine exactly what form his help takes, or why, with a household filled to bursting with maids and footmen, it is needed.

The ball is tomorrow, and this morning he left for Rosings directly after we breakfasted. I have been playing with Louisa all morning while Martha helps Mrs. Baxter with the laundry, but now Louisa is napping and I am unable to settle to any useful work, thoughts of tomorrow evening plucking at my mind and distracting me from the sewing in my lap. I rise and steal upstairs on my toes, hoping the creaking of the steps does not rouse Louisa. In my bedchamber, I open the clothespress and look down at my new gown. It was an extravagance suggested by William, though I made only a token protest about the unnecessary expense. Both of us, it seems, are vain enough to want me to look my best, though a part of me worries that—despite William's assurances that my position requires elegance of dress—in making so much effort, I will merely look ridiculous among the tenants' much simpler Sunday best. And it is with no small amount of shame that I know my desire to look well is only increased because I've no wish to look especially dowdy beside Elizabeth.

The gown is prettier than any I have worn in a long while, the lutestring dyed the pale gray-green of sage leaves. When I dithered over fabrics at the draper's, the young woman working there held this fabric up before me and declared that it was just the color to complement my hair and complexion. It is strange, at thirty, to feel so like a young girl looking forward to her first dance—that peculiar blend of nervousness and excitement and pure possibility—and of course, my first dance was not the triumph I had envisioned.

I reach out, touch the gown with one fingertip, then snatch my hand back and shut the clothespress decisively. Some feelings, I think, are better not examined too closely.

WILLIAM CALLS TO me from downstairs, his voice sounding as anxious as I feel. I take one last look in the glass, convinced that I must have disordered myself somehow, but I am still neat in my new gown, my hair smooth under a narrow ribbon bandeau. Then I touch my pearls where they lie against my collarbone, their warmth a comfort beneath my palm, and leave the room.

William is waiting at the foot of the stairs. He looks harried, and he says nothing about my appearance, only offers me his arm.

We arrive at Rosings to find the great hall brightly lit. "The expense," William whispers to me, gleeful, as he looks around us. "Just think of the expense!" I can nearly hear his mind tallying the number of candles. Though the ball has not yet formally begun, Lady Catherine's tenants already fill the space. They stand in clusters, dressed in their best clothes, chattering with excitement and furtively looking around themselves at the opulent room.

William nods this way and that in acknowledgment of greetings but leads me unerringly to where her ladyship sits with Miss de Bourgh. Elizabeth, Mr. Darcy, and Mrs. Jenkinson stand beside the ladies of Rosings. We make our bows, and as we rise William says, "The hall is glorious, Your Ladyship! I imagine your tenants will be speaking of nothing else for weeks."

"I should certainly think so," Lady Catherine says. She turns her attention upon me. "Mrs. Collins, I am pleased that you are able to attend. Your confinement last year was most inconvenient."

"I am very happy to be here, Lady Catherine."

She nods, but her expression is peevish. "If Anne were stronger, she would lead the dancing," she says. "Had it not been for her illness, she would be a *most* accomplished dancer." We all, as one, look at Miss de Bourgh, who sits in her chair like an unstarched gown. She gazes down at her lap, as though unaware of our inspection.

"Indeed," William says, "we must all feel the deprivation— to watch Miss de Bourgh dance would surely be the greatest of pleasures. Her grace would be recognized by all, her—"

"Mrs. Darcy," Lady Catherine interrupts, "you must lead the dancing in Anne's stead. Mr. Collins will partner you."

"You do me great honor, Your Ladyship," William says, and bows deeply to Elizabeth, who turns away to hide her smile. I pretend not to notice, looking instead at the hall, paneled walls glowing with soft light, tables laden with food for the supper that will come after the dancing. The air is thick with the heat of so many bodies and with the excitement of anticipation. Musicians stand ready in the corner; one draws his bow across the strings of his fiddle, a single long, high note, then adjusts something at the neck of the instrument. My eyes sweep across the familiar faces in the crowd, cottagers and tradesmen and farmers . . .

I do not acknowledge to myself whose face it is that I am seeking until the moment I find it, half-turned aside and most of the way across the long room, and my blood begins to rush queerly in my ears.

Mr. Travis's dark hair is unusually tidy, and he wears a coat I have not seen before. I let myself see these things and then I turn away, look back at Lady Catherine in her high-backed chair with her mouth curled up and her eyes sharp. She makes a gesture and the musicians begin tuning their instruments in earnest. William turns to Elizabeth.

"Mrs. Darcy," he says, and Elizabeth, her face impressively blank, looks neither at me nor at her husband as she allows herself to be led onto the floor. I step back, nearer to Mrs. Jenkinson's place beside Miss de Bourgh's chair. A murmur runs through the crowd; a few brave couples join the set. Lizzy calls the dance.

There is nothing like a dance to change the energy in a room; I feel the notes of the song in my fingertips and toes. I hear so little music, here in Kent, beyond a performance, now and again, on the pianoforte at Rosings. The dancers move through the figures with more enthusiasm than expertise— even Lizzy, encumbered by William, is less graceful than I remember her being—but it is a merry song, and enthusiasm, really, is all that is required. My feet tap lightly against the polished floor, hidden by the hem of my gown and soundless in their soft slippers.

"Mrs. Collins, you should be dancing," Lady Catherine says. She leans forward in her chair, reaches out and catches at her nephew's sleeve. "Darcy—set an example."

My hands twitch, and I hide them in the folds of my skirt.

Mr. Darcy's shoulders are one tense line. "Your Ladyship," I say, "it has been a long while since I last danced—"

She frowns. "I am sure you have not forgotten how, Mrs. Collins."

Mr. Darcy turns to me, hand extended. "Will you do me the honor?"

I am embarrassed for both of us. "Thank you." I can feel the eyes of the parishioners upon us as we take our place at the end of the line; I keep my own eyes on Mr. Darcy's waistcoat, not allowing myself to look about and see who, exactly, is watching us, until the moment comes to enter the dance. And then there is nothing but movement and music, people coming together and flinging apart. I had almost forgotten the heady rush of so many bodies, the heat generated among us, the din of stamping feet and clapping hands. The steps return to me quickly, and Mr. Darcy, for all his reluctance in a ballroom, is an excellent dancer. When the set has ended, I am out of breath and giddy with it. Mr. Darcy offers his hand, leads me from the floor.

"Charlotte!" comes Lizzy's voice. We turn; she and William hurry toward us. Lizzy looks less exhilarated than I feel, and she drops William's hand the moment she politely can, looking at Mr. Darcy. "I wondered how soon Lady Catherine would have you dancing."

Mr. Darcy's smile is pained. "She chose a fine partner, at least," he says, with a half bow in my direction.

I doubt whether Lady Catherine will insist on her nephew's dancing again, for I cannot imagine she wishes to see him partnered with farmers' daughters or tradesmen's wives. But it would be impolitic to say so—though if I were having this conversation with someone else, I mightn't be sensible enough to censor myself. I glance over to the corner where Mr. Travis was standing earlier; he is still there. He sees me looking, smiles just a little. I nod, feel my lips pull up in response, and look away again.

"Speaking of my aunt, I should be dutiful and see if she or my cousin needs anything." Mr. Darcy looks from Elizabeth to me and raises his voice, for the music is starting again. "Would either of you like refreshment?"

"No, thank you," I say, and Eliza shakes her head. He bows, turns, and begins to weave his way through the crowd. I look at William, hovering behind Lizzy's elbow.

"My dear," I say, "perhaps you ought to attend her ladyship as well."

He seems relieved. "Yes! Of course. An excellent idea." He turns around a little too quickly and nearly stumbles over the feet of a passing woman. I keep my face very still, listening to his stuttered apologies, and then Lizzy turns to me.

"I was surprised when Darcy told me that there is a tradition of holding a harvest ball at Rosings," she says, bending her head close to mine. "It did not seem very like Lady Catherine to willingly mingle with her tenants."

William has moved far enough away now that the music and conversation around us have drowned out the sound of his voice. I make my own voice light and teasing. "But you are forgetting her famous generosity."

She laughs. "How foolish of me. Of course. I—" But then she stops, her attention caught by something just over my shoulder. I turn, and there is Mr. Travis only a few paces away. His posture speaks of indecision, but he sees us looking and bows immediately.

"I apologize, Mrs. Collins," he says. "I did not mean to interrupt."

"Not at all." My voice sounds thin, and I resist the urge to clear my throat. "Elizabeth, may I introduce Mr. Travis? Mr. Travis, my friend Mrs. Darcy."

He bows again, and Lizzy does likewise, rising with an expression of polite curiosity.

"Mr. Travis planted the roses for us," I say, for want of something better.

"Oh, yes—Mr. Collins was very eager to show them off," Elizabeth says. She smiles her easy smile, and my teeth grind together. "How kind of you to offer your time and expertise."

Mr. Travis chuckles, glances at me, and rubs the back of his neck.

"It was nothing, ma'am," he says, and then, "I truly did not mean to interrupt—it is only that I have strict orders from my father, Mrs. Collins, to give you his greetings, and I did not know whether I would have another opportunity."

"Oh—I *am* sorry he is unable to be here."

"As is he." More people are crowding about; he edges a little nearer, jostled by a passing couple. "This was always his favorite event of the year."

"Please tell him I will call with Louisa very soon—well, after we return from Hertfordshire," I say, but then Mr. Clifton, whose estate lies two miles from Rosings, steps forward out of the crowd and bows low to Elizabeth. His bald head gleams in the light of so many candles.

"Might we dance this one, Mrs. Darcy?"

She takes his hand. "I—yes, thank you," she says, and follows him to the floor with a quick, startled look back at me.

"You go to Hertfordshire soon, then?"

I am very aware of Mr. Travis's nearness, and I keep my eyes on Eliza and Mr. Clifton, who stand awaiting the start of the music. "Yes—in but a few days. But we will not stay long. Only a fortnight."

"I am sorry you will have so little time with your family, though—" He breaks off and I do look at him now. He is frowning at the forming set, but he must feel me eyeing him, for he turns a little in my direction.

"You are a fine dancer, Mrs. Collins," he says abruptly. "You seemed to be enjoying yourself very much."

He watched, I think, and then do not let myself think of it any further. "Yes," I say. "I missed it more than I realized."

He half-smiles and looks again at the lined-up couples. "I would follow Mr. Clifton's example and ask you to dance," he says, "but I suppose doing so would be seen as something of a presumption."

My lips part. There is nothing in the world I want more than to be part of the fray with him, a partner with whom I could be at ease. With whom I could laugh. I imagine our hands touching and our bodies moving together with the music. The longing to accept batters me. But: just a little ways away, Mrs. Prewitt and her niece are standing, also watching the dancers assemble; I think of Mrs. Prewitt's words outside the church and suddenly I cannot breathe. I look at Mr. Travis's face, still turned toward the dance, at the lines at the corners of his eyes, the bit of tightness at the corners of his mouth, and I wonder how I can possibly step back from this friendship that has grown so easily, seemingly from nothing.

But perhaps it is arrogant to think that he would mind if our conversations dwindled away, if we met at church or by chance in the village and exchanged only indifferent greetings. Perhaps the prospect of retreating into cold civility would not leave him sore and aching.

Then I look at his fingers, knotted together hard behind his back, and my mind goes blank and silent.

Miss Harmon is smiling anxiously at nothing in particular. There is a wrenching inside of me, and I say, in a voice that is too falsely bright to really be mine, "If you truly wish to dance, Mr. Travis, I see a young lady in need of a partner." I tilt my head in Miss Harmon's direction.

Mr. Travis opens his mouth, glances in the direction I have indicated, and closes it again. "I . . . Of course."

I am conscious of his presence behind me as I make my way over to Mrs. Prewitt and her niece.

"Mrs. Collins!" Mrs. Prewitt says. She flicks a look at Mr. Travis. "What a fine occasion this is!"

"Yes, indeed," I say, and to Miss Harmon, "May I introduce Mr. Travis to you, Miss Harmon?"

She looks at him, smiles prettily. "It would be my pleasure."

I make the introduction quickly. "Miss Harmon is visiting from the north," I tell Mr. Travis.

"Oh, yes?" He turns to her, all polite attention. "That must have been quite a journey."

"It was. But it is very good to see my aunt and uncle."

He says, "Would you care to dance?" She agrees, and he offers her his arm. Then he bows swiftly to Mrs. Prewitt and myself. "Excuse us, ladies," he says, with one quick, unreadable look at me, and they join the set.

"A fine beginning," Mrs. Prewitt says from beside me. "They do look well together, don't they, Mrs. Collins?"

Miss Harmon dances beautifully, and Mr. Travis, though less light-footed than Mr. Darcy, moves with confidence. Their hands clasp in the course of the dance, and then they part, twirling away from each other. And then they return. A headache threatens suddenly, just between my eyes.

"Yes," I say. "They do look very well."

Chapter Nineteen

Maria must have been waiting at the parlor window, for the coach has not even rolled to a stop when she comes bursting through the front door to stand, body drawn tight with impatience, upon the drive. William alights first, then helps me down; I scarcely set both feet upon the ground before my sister has enveloped both me and Louisa in a crushing embrace.

"It is *so* good to see you!" she says. "And oh, sweet niece, you are so big!"

I find that I am blinking against sudden tears. It has been so long since I have seen her—more than ten months since her last visit to Kent. She smells just as I remember from years of sharing a bed.

William clears his throat, and Maria and I pull apart. She looks at him guiltily. "Sister," he says, and holds out his hand.

She places hers in it and he bows with exaggerated gallantry. "Though she does not entirely approve of your choice of husband," he says as he rises, "Lady Catherine sent us from Rosings Park with her felicitations." He presses her hand and releases it.

I close my eyes, but not in time to miss the way Maria's face turns scarlet. "I—" she says, and then my parents and youngest brothers are hurrying through the doorway, saving her from the necessity of an appropriate response to so inappropriate a statement.

"Mr. Collins!" my mother says. She kisses his cheek, and William flushes rosier than Maria. And then my mother turns to me; her gaze darts between my face and Louisa's, and she laughs and says, "I hardly know whom I missed most!" and wraps us both in her arms. A moment later and she is stepping back, but she reaches for Louisa. "Let me see you, my big girl," she says, but Louisa leans back in her arms.

"Ma!" she says. "Ma! Ma!" She holds out her hands to me.

"Oh, hush now," my mother says, and begins walking toward the house. "I have taken out all of your mamma and auntie's old toys, they have been waiting impatiently for you to arrive and play with them."

My chest feels full and warm as I watch them go. And now my father is standing before me. His hair has turned fully gray, but his smile is exactly the same. "Charlotte," he says, and leans down to kiss my cheek. He smells the same, too, the crisp lemon scent of the cologne he always applies a little too strongly.

"Father." It is silly, perhaps, to be so utterly consumed by gladness, but I am *home*, and my brothers Samuel and Frederick are waiting their turns to greet me, having already shaken William's hand with great solemnity. "You have grown so!" I say—Frederick, who is still so young in my mind, sports a few wisps of hair above his upper lip—and they both shuffle their feet and grin.

DINNER IS TO be a far noisier affair than I'd have chosen, for my mother invited the Bennets and the Longs to dine with us. This means that Maria and I are both drafted into service, my mother passing Louisa off to William with a casual "She is all yours for a few hours, Mr. Collins!" She either does not notice or chooses to ignore the flash of panic that crosses his face as she pulls me toward the kitchen.

"There will be four courses," my mother says. She wraps an apron around my waist as though I am still a little girl who cannot tie the strings herself. Maria covers her mouth but cannot hide the laughter at the corners of her eyes.

Most of the preparation was already finished yesterday, of course, but there is still plenty to do. Maria busies herself arranging fruit while our mother and I ready chicken and hares for cooking. "When do I get to meet the famed Mr. Cowper?" I say.

Maria's smile says a great deal. "Did I forget to mention—he will join us tonight."

I glance at our mother, whose face is set stoically. "He sounds like an amiable man," I say.

"You will adore him, Charlotte," Maria says. "He is so very good."

Our mother releases her breath on a sigh quiet enough that I do not think Maria could have heard it.

"Do you not like Mr. Cowper?" I say in a whisper when Maria goes to fetch something from the larder.

"Oh, he is a good enough sort of man. And he does seem very fond of your sister. But his profession, Charlotte . . . An apothecary! Maria's head has always been filled with fancies. If only she were sensible like you."

"He can provide for her though, surely?"

"After a fashion. But she will never live up to our hopes for her now, and that's a fact."

Maria returns bearing a large platter, and so I must hold my peace.

MR. COWPER IS a very handsome man of six-and-twenty, with a classical face and curling hair. He and Maria make an attractive couple. When the maid leads him into the parlor before dinner, he makes his bows to my mother and father, but he looks unerringly to Maria where she stands talking to

Mrs. Long. They greet each other with their eyes before they are able to speak to one another. I look away.

Mr. Cowper and I are seated together at dinner. He is attentive and eager to please, if rather quiet, and several times I look up to find Maria watching him with an expression of great affection from across the table.

"My sister speaks very highly of you," I say. "I should thank you, sir, for making her so happy."

"It is she who has made me happy, Mrs. Collins."

I smile. "That was just the right response," I say, and he laughs. But we have little chance to speak further.

Like my father, Mr. Bennet looks older than in my memories, his white hair thinner and his waistline thicker. He has been mostly silent throughout dinner, leaving the burden of conversation to his wife, who has cheerfully taken it up—she has managed to mention her eldest daughters' illustrious marriages at least ten times since the first course. I am almost too tired to be amused; if only my mother had waited until a day or two after our arrival to hold a party.

Mrs. Bennet leans across the table. "Did you think Lizzy looked well when she was in Kent?" she says to me, and then, before I can respond, she adds for the benefit of any who might not have already known the information, "Mr. and Mrs. Darcy were lately invited to be guests of Lady Catherine de Bourgh of Rosings Park."

Mr. Bennet rolls his eyes and takes a deep drink from his glass.

"She looked remarkably well," I say, "and little Thomas is quite the handsome boy."

Mrs. Bennet smiles widely. "Her pin money alone could keep all my girls in gowns and slippers forever. I had hoped Kitty could stay with her at Pemberley for the summer, but Lizzy said not, and I suppose with a new baby she mightn't have as much time to find her younger sister a husband as I would like. So Kitty has been with Jane and Mr. Bingley at their estate for two months now. Jane writes that Kitty has been much admired." She plucks an almond from its dish and pops it in her mouth, chews for a moment, and adds, with a pointed little look at Maria, "There is nothing like an advantageous marriage to ease a mother's mind."

I glance at Mr. Cowper, who is attending to his lemon cream with apparent single-mindedness.

My mother's eyes narrow, but she says only, "Indeed. Which is why Charlotte's wedding to Mr. Collins brought such gladness to us all, knowing that one day she will be mistress of Longbourn estate." She nods to Mr. Bennet. "One day far in the future we hope, of course."

Mr. Bennet's smile is sardonic. "Oh, I've been informed by my wife that now Jane and Lizzy are settled I may die as soon as I choose. She has her pick of grand estates in which to spend the rest of her days." He raises his glass to William.

"Your inheritance holds no terrors for us any longer, Mr. Collins."

William blinks. "I am glad to hear it, sir—you know that I was always uneasy about it, and would have made amends had I been able. But circumstances, ah, being what they were . . ."

I long to kick him into silence, but he is too far away down the table, and so I settle for a generous sip of my own wine.

THE DAYS HAVE passed in a whirl of calls made and received, between which I spend most of my time in the parlor with Maria and our mother, helping them finish a few last items for my sister's trousseau.

My father and William do whatever it is that men do in one another's company. I cannot imagine what they might find to talk about, other than the splendor of Rosings Park. And my brothers spend their days at school. I see them but rarely, and when I do I never know what to say to them.

My eldest brother is off term at Oxford, where he is studying the law, a fact that my mother has managed to work into conversation with nearly everyone we meet. She lingers over the word *Oxford* as if it were a sugared confection. We had always assumed that my eldest brother would take over our father's shop when he was old enough; with the shop sold, that option was lost to him, but in its place was our father's determination that his sons should be educated as gentlemen.

Listening to my mother's quiet boasting, I am struck by sudden understanding: her feelings about our family's rise in status are as complicated as my own, her vanity warring with her natural practicality. She is proud that my brother will one day be a barrister, rather than a merchant or a lowly solicitor, and she loves to talk about my eventual role as the mistress of Longbourn—an extraordinary stroke of luck, which would certainly never have happened were I still the daughter of a shopkeeper. But when my father was a merchant, our family was prosperous, if not genteel, and my mother had no worries. My brothers could have gone into trade without any loss of status, and Maria could have married Mr. Cowper without her choice being seen as a degradation.

My brother had been staying with a friend but returned home last night for the wedding. He, too, has grown so much since I saw him last; I must tip my head back to look into his eyes. I can almost imagine him as a London barrister, someone who might attract a wife with a fine dowry. To my delight, he seems very taken with Louisa, though he disappeared this afternoon with some childhood friends, despite my mother's protestations that it looked like rain.

"Boys," she said. She shook her head and watched him go. "And two more left to raise." It began to rain steadily not a quarter hour after he left.

Today is the day before the wedding. A little while ago, my mother took Louisa with her into the kitchen; I am embroidering a reticule while Maria alternates between adding lace to a cap and gazing out the window with a furrow between her brows.

"I do hope the rain stops soon," she says, and stabs her needle into the cap's fabric. Then she raises her head yet again, watching as the rain falls against the glass in sheets. "Though I suppose it will make little difference whether it stops now or tonight; it will be a muddy walk to the church tomorrow either way."

"It is not the weather but the ceremony which matters tomorrow," I say.

She exhales her frustration. "I know! But would it be too much to ask that the weather reflect the happiness of the occasion?"

I laugh. "It cannot be fine on every bride's wedding day, or we would never have any rain at all."

"Yes, but not every bride's wedding day is a happy one," she says, and I feel my smile slip away. She does not notice, but holds up the cap. "Do you think this will become me? I have tried on all my others, and I confess I cannot decide whether I look well in them or not."

The cap is made of insubstantial material, with fine lace at the edges. The cap I am wearing just now is very plain in comparison. "Of course it will become you," I say. "Very few things would not, I think, and something as pretty as that cannot help but look well."

She smiles and returns to her work. The steady pounding of rain on the walls and windows is the only sound in the room. When Maria speaks again, she startles me. "Would it be too strange to ask you to sleep with me tonight?" she says.

I look at her. "Maria," I say, but she reaches forward and captures my hand.

"Oh, please do," she says. "I know I shall be too nervous to sleep much, and we could talk as we used to."

I think of our old bed, with its warm soft coverlet and the familiar dips in the mattress where each of us lay. "I would like that very much."

She starts to smile. "Mr. Collins would not object?"

I have no idea what William will make of this, but I say, "Not in the least."

WILLIAM MADE A few bleating objections to Maria's and my plan but was silenced by my talk of sisterly duty and devotion, so I now find myself tucked into bed beside my sister for the first time in years. The rain has subsided into a light, arrhythmic patter on the roof, and the single candle on the night table casts dancing shadows upon the walls. The sound of my sister's breathing, the pillow under my head, the pattern of the paper-hangings are all so familiar. It feels like I am in a dream world, hushed and still, where the colors are not as bright as they should be.

Maria turns on her side to look at me.

"I am so happy, Charlotte," she whispers.

"Then I am glad for you."

"You do like him?"

I am happy to be able to answer truthfully. "Very much."

"Is it . . . Mamma told me something of what to expect, of course, but—is it all right? What happens . . . between a husband and wife, I mean."

My body is hot and prickly, and I am grateful for the faint, flickering light. "It is nothing to fear," I say.

She blows out a relieved breath. "George wants ever so many children."

"And they will doubtless all be little cherubs, with your coloring and his curls," I say, smiling.

"If they are half as sweet as my niece, I will be content."

I prop myself on my elbow. "May I ask—your courtship was so short. So—sudden. Until you wrote to me of Mr. Cowper, the last man you spoke of was Mr. Andrews, who asked you twice to dance. How . . . what made you sure of Mr. Cowper?"

She is giving me a most peculiar look. "It was no faster or more sudden than your engagement. But, well . . . I cannot really explain it. When George and I spoke it was—easy. He understood what I was saying." She shakes her head. "I must sound very silly."

There are dark eyes and crooked teeth and a gentle smile in my head; I cannot get them out. "No," I say. "Not silly."

She gives a little laugh. "And I never really liked Mr. Andrews—he has the largest ears you have ever seen, and he is so much shorter than I am—it was like dancing with Frederick."

Again, that prickling heat. "A man needn't be handsome to be worthy of your attention," I say.

She flinches back from my vehemence, cups her palm over her mouth. "Of course not," she says through her fingers, and then puts out her other hand to touch my arm. "I am sorry—that was thoughtless of me. Even men who are not so well favored can make excellent husbands."

She thinks I am talking about William—naturally, she does. I roll onto my back and her hand slides away from my arm.

"Do not let us quarrel," she says. "Please, Charlotte."

There is something the matter with me. I stare up at the canopy until the pattern of the fabric there blurs before my eyes. "There is nothing to quarrel about," I say. "I should not have taken offense; I am only tired."

I can hear her swallow. "Of course."

I must do better than this. I force myself to turn back toward her. "Truly, Maria—I am so glad for you."

Her smile starts small but spreads quickly, and she scoots nearer to me. "I have not even told you about his proposal," she says, and I lean forward to listen.

THE CHURCH PORCH is strewn with herbs and rushes. Our feet crush them as we enter, releasing a scent pungent enough to compete with the smell of damp grass. The rain stopped sometime during the night, though we had a time protecting Maria's slippers and hem from the muddy lane as we walked to the church. But the sun is shining weakly through the clouds.

Chapter Twenty

It is nearly evening when we reach the parsonage. Louisa wriggles in my arms as William leaves the coach, wailing her impatience to be free. The moment I set her upon the ground, she is running, weaving like a drunkard through the hedgerows.

John is taking our luggage from the driver, while William says something in a peevish voice. I untie the ribbons under my chin and remove my bonnet, bending my head to let the cool air drift across the back of my neck. My hairpins pinch, and I wish it were time to go upstairs and remove them, to take off this gown and the corset underneath and lie down in my nightshift. I look up at the house. Its stone walls, its neatly placed windows and stout chimneys, are so familiar. Mrs. Baxter has opened the front door and is standing to the side, waiting for us to come in so she can take our outer garments.

I think of my parents' maid, throwing open the door to Lucas Lodge as the wedding party returned after the service. She smiled and bobbed curtsies and clasped Maria's free hand, the one not wrapped possessively around Mr. Cowper's arm, and said, "I'm so glad for you, Miss—"

And then she'd clapped a hand over her own mouth, her grin growing wide behind her fingers. "I mean, *Mrs. Cowper*," she said. Maria blushed and smiled shyly up at her new husband.

We all sat down to a handsome wedding breakfast, which Gabby, my mother, Maria, and I had begun preparing the day before. The cake was rich with nuts and dried fruit, covered with icing flavored with almonds and rose water. I offered bites to Louisa from my own plate as William, seated a little down the table, compared it favorably to a cake he had enjoyed, at the wedding of the Cliftons' daughter, when he first arrived in Kent. "Lady Catherine," he said, "spoke very approvingly of the flavor."

My mother accepted this highest of compliments with obvious pleasure. Her dismay over Mr. Cowper's profession seemed entirely forgotten, at least for the moment; at the church, as the couple stood rapt before the vicar, I had watched my mother watch them. She must have felt my gaze, for she turned to me and smiled a little.

"I suppose they do look well together," she had whispered, her lips barely moving, and my thoughts were thrown abruptly back to the harvest ball, Mrs. Prewitt saying the very same words to me as we watched her niece dancing with Mr. Travis.

"And happy," my mother had said after a moment—so softly that I was unsure whether she spoke to me or to herself—and I dragged my mind forcibly back to the present, to Mr. Cowper standing straight and handsome, looking down upon my sister with shining gladness; to Maria, looking up at him with a secret sort of smile. The damp made Maria's hair curl becomingly around the autumn flowers woven through it from our parents' garden. I cast a quick look across the church, to where Mr. Cowper's parents and sister sat; his mother was crying, his father patting her hand.

We all drank to the couple's health and fruitfulness before they left for Mr. Cowper's—now their—home. My father spoke at length, and with great feeling and self-importance, welcoming the Cowpers into his home and into his family. The room felt saturated with goodwill, and for the first time I almost regretted my choice to forgo a feast after my own wedding. But perhaps the mood would have been different, my parents' pride in my conquest shadowed by my own ambivalence. But this feast, at least, was quite unspoiled. Louisa was passed from person to person like a squirming parcel, and I watched as my parents, my sister, even my brothers kissed and petted her. Even William, full of cake and fruit and wine, had subsided into happy silence.

Now I back away from the parsonage, slowly at first, and then more quickly until I am nearly running, my bonnet in one hand and my breath hindered by a crushing pressure inside my chest. I spy Louisa darting down a path; she squeals when she sees me, and a little of the pressure eases as I turn around so I can give chase properly. There is no need to go inside just yet.

THE HEAT INSIDE the church is unseasonably oppressive, dense with the moisture that heralds a coming storm. At his pulpit, William is sweating heavily in his stock and cassock, his hair plastered to his forehead and in front of his ears. Though I oughtn't be, I am grateful that so few congregants have attended this morning's service, for the press and heat of more bodies would be intolerable. As it is, I wish William would shorten his sermon; but improvisation is not one of his strengths.

It feels like release when the service is finally ended, the hot stagnant air inside the church seeping like treacle through the thrown-open doors. I stand outside and welcome the warm wind against my cheeks. We are all listless, our greetings less animated than usual. Even Lady Catherine is subdued; no doubt she feels the disadvantage of her gown's heavy fabric beside the thin muslins of the other women's dresses. William mops his brow with a handkerchief and accepts thanks from the churchgoers with rounded shoulders and modest smiles.

I allow myself to be drawn into conversation with Mrs. Jenkinson. At the edge of my vision I can see Mr. Travis standing, speaking with another man; I know, from the slight turn of his head, that he is watching me, too. Though I want to, I do not excuse myself, even when the other man walks away and Mr. Travis is alone. Instead, I stay where I am, safely ensconced among the party from Rosings. The wind twists my skirts around my legs, and I hold my elbows and pretend to study the gathering clouds.

THE RAIN BEGINS to rush down just after we return to the parsonage—the door has not yet closed behind us when there is a crash of thunder and a sudden deluge. Both William and I turn in surprise, framed in the doorway and watching as our small courtyard turns, very quickly, to mud. Louisa, startled by the thunder, clutches at my neck.

William is the first of us to stir. "I was going to walk to Rosings to offer my help in the gardens," he says, and looks up at the sky, where the clouds have drawn together into a solid mass. Then he turns to me. "Shall we keep each other company, my dear? What were your plans for the afternoon?"

With Martha with her family, and the rain falling so heavily, there is nothing to do but stay with Louisa in the nursery. I say so, and William looks at our daughter as though surprised to find her there, then down the hall toward his book room, and then up again at the sky. My shoulders grow taut at the idea of being shut up with him and all his nervous energy.

"An excellent notion," he says.

Upstairs, William stands with his hands at his sides as he watches Louisa chase her spinning top across the floor, quick and graceless on her hands and knees, squealing her excitement. I wish, perhaps unkindly, that he would leave us alone. When she notices his observation she looks up at him with a sort of wary curiosity; his lips curl into an uncertain smile; and then she is distracted when the top stops spinning and tumbles onto its side.

MRS. BAXTER TURNS the meat near the fire, then wipes her brow with one brawny forearm. It is unbearably hot in the kitchen, even after yesterday's storm and with the door open to let in the breeze. I can feel my chemise and dress clinging to my back. Fat drips from the joint into the pan beneath, and there is a sizzle and hiss. Mrs. Baxter sighs.

Life has felt strange and stagnant in the days since we returned to Kent. I have been spending much of my time in the kitchen with Mrs. Baxter. The trees and bushes and the plants in the kitchen garden are heavily laden with fruits and vegetables that must be harvested and preserved to keep through the winter. I made a cask of elderberry wine before we departed for Maria's wedding, but there is still mead to make from William's honey, and jars and jars of jams and pickles to put up. And all the while, Mrs. Baxter and I scarcely speak a word to one another. I am sure William would approve; he is very much in favor of servants knowing their place. But after being at home, where the kitchen work was passed in animated conversation with my mother, my sister, and even the maid, the quiet hours here pass very slowly.

There is one person with whom I would particularly like to speak, but despite having several times ventured out to visit parishioners since our return, I have put off calling at the Travis farm, though I know I must call soon so that old Mr. Travis can enjoy some time with Louisa.

Instead, I imagine conversations with the younger Mr. Travis as I pack cabbage and cauliflower into jars; I have spoken more to him in my head in the fortnight since our return than I have in reality to anyone else. I describe dinner with the Bennets on our first night in Hertfordshire and hear his low laugh; he listens attentively when I describe Maria's wedding and my relief at discovering that Mr. Cowper seemed a very agreeable, gentlemanlike man.

But I feel frozen whenever I think about meeting him somewhere in public; I do not know that I can bring myself to be merely civil, as I have determined I must be.

"It seems impossible that it is autumn, and not the height of summer," I venture.

"Indeed, ma'am," Mrs. Baxter says, and then our conversation lapses once more. I try vainly to think of something more to say. The housekeeper fans herself with her apron and looks about for her next task, seeming quite unconcerned by the littleness of our exchanges. I close my eyes against the smokiness of the fire. The meat spits again; again, Mrs. Baxter sighs.

IN THE VILLAGE, Mr. Travis is speaking to the blacksmith. I keep my face mostly averted as I go about my shopping so as to avoid the necessity of deciding how best to greet him. But I needn't have worried; he is cornered almost immediately by Mrs. Prewitt, her niece pulled along behind her.

WE ARE INVITED to Rosings for the evening. The Cliftons are coming with their son, who is home from Cambridge, and Lady Catherine's note indicated that our presence was required so there would be the proper number of people for quadrille after dinner.

"How well you look this evening, my dear," William says as we walk the short distance down the lane.

I look at him. "I—thank you," I say, and then look away again. William is a great payer of compliments, but I know for a fact that the two ladies he wished to marry before he proposed to me—before turning his attentions to Lizzy, he admired her elder sister, Jane, until it became obvious that Jane and our neighbor, Mr. Bingley, had already formed an attachment—were both very handsome. I find it hard to trust his words.

Dinner is the usual refined affair, and I am silent throughout much of it, eating and drinking only a little and watching those around me. The dining room at Rosings is lit by dozens of candles, but still it is so vast that much of the room remains in darkness, the footmen lining the walls merely man-shaped shadows except when they step forward to pour wine. The candles do, however, illuminate the gleaming table settings and platters of rich foods, and cast the faces of my dining companions in a light that gentles all of their profiles and makes even William almost handsome.

The conversation, if it can truly be called such, is propelled largely by Lady Catherine and requires little participation from the rest of us. She dispenses advice like an apothecary's draughts, and I wonder with sudden tiredness whether the others at the table are nodding and smiling with as little sincerity as I am. I want, very badly all of a sudden, to be away from here, and I press my feet in their thin slippers hard against the floor to keep myself still.

There seems to be something blocking my throat; I take a little wine, but it merely trickles around the blockage, and there is something pressing on my chest, too, and a buzzing in my head that dulls the voices around me to a faint murmur. To either side of me, Mr. Clifton and Mrs. Jenkinson are eating their pigeon with apparent relish, and I watch them with a strange sense of disconnectedness. I look into the flickering flames of the many-armed candelabra at the center of the table, and cannot breathe.

Chapter Twenty-One

Louisa and I go outside at dawn. Travel seems to have disturbed her sleep schedule, and so she and I have been rising together once more. The morning is chilly; I wrap us both in a warm shawl but do not bother to change out of my nightdress or do anything else except don my boots. William would be horrified, but he will not be awake for hours yet.

The sky is streaked with orange and pink. I point out the colors to Louisa, push the hair that has escaped its plait behind my ears. She fidgets until I let her down, and then she runs unerringly toward the pig's pen and stands staring at the animal where it lies upon the ground, twitching in its sleep. In a very few weeks it will be fat enough to slaughter, and then she will have to wait until next spring for us to get another. I stand back, arms wrapped around myself, and watch her.

Though the garden is still blooming, the blossoms are growing blowsy and losing petals; the sun, rising swiftly now, is still bright, but there is a particular smell to the air, sharp as autumn, like damp leaves underfoot even though they have yet to turn and fall. The world is in transition, and I stand inert as it changes around me.

It was not so long ago that I stood in this garden with my hair in disarray and my baby in my arms and came upon a strange man removing a tree stump. I look down at myself, at the thin fabric of my nightgown, then over my shoulder self-consciously; but of course there is no one there.

I HAVE COME halfway down the stairs after laying Louisa down for the night when William hurries into the hall. He is all nervousness, and I pause, watching; he holds his prayer book in one hand and retrieves his hat from its peg with the other. When he reaches for the latch, I say, "William," and he gives a great start, turning to look at me.

"Where are you going?" I say. It is nearly time for dinner, and he knows I ordered his favorite soup this evening.

"Mr. Travis's lad just arrived," he says. "I am needed there."

"Needed . . . ," I say; my voice comes out as a wheeze.

"The elder Mr. Travis was . . . stricken during the night. He has not been able to make the walk to church for some time; I must go and administer Communion and hear his confession."

My hands fly to my mouth. "Oh, no—"

"Do not hold dinner; I do not know how long this will take."

My words are reflexive, for I am entirely numb. "I will have Mrs. Baxter keep something warm for you."

"Thank you, my dear," William says. He has tucked his prayer book under his arm and is turning his hat over and over in his hands. I look away, uncomfortable with his discomfort. William is not well suited to the role of consoler of the dying.

He moves to go once more, and I look back at him. The words seem to throw themselves from my mouth. "I will go with you."

William looks puzzled. "Charlotte—that is unnecessary."

I curl my fingers around the handrail. "But—"

"No, no—you must stay here. I am sure the thought was kindly meant, but . . ." He waves a hand at me and opens the door. The rest of his sentence is lost to his own distraction; he puts his hat on his head and closes the door behind him. My eyes are burning. I sink slowly down upon the stair and remain there until Mrs. Baxter finds me to say that dinner is ready and waiting.

I AM IN bed when I hear the knell of the church bell. Nine slow, solemn peals, and then silence. I weep, face pressed into my pillow, fingers clutching at the bedclothes.

When William comes to bed, I am still awake. I lie quietly, my grief spent, as he settles in beside me—he breathes loudly, shifting this way and that until he is comfortable—and wait for him to speak, but he only looks surprised to find me watching him, and squeezes my fingers together beneath the quilt.

"You should be asleep," he says, closing his eyes.

"Wait," I say, and he looks at me. It is dark enough that I cannot see his annoyance clearly. "What happened? Mr. Travis is—"

"He has ascended from this place," William says. I feel again the sudden tightness at my temples and behind my jaw. I hold my lips together and swallow several times.

"Was it—peaceful?" I say at last. William stirs.

"He was insensible, for the most part, and too weak to take Communion." William presses his thumb and forefinger into the inner corners of his eyes. "Though he could not speak to express it, I flatter myself that I gave him great comfort, in the end."

Agitation comes over me; I curl my toes against the mattress to hold myself in place. "And his son?" I say, more sharply than I intended.

"We will hold the funeral as soon as the coffin can be made," he says, which does not answer my question. I stare at the ceiling; dampness trickles from the corner of one eye and down my temple, pooling uncomfortably in my ear.

"Who is readying the body?" I say. As far as I know, Mr. Travis has no female relatives living.

William yawns. "He will send his lad for the midwife in the morning, I imagine. Or perhaps his maid; it was not something we discussed."

Of course. I think of Mrs. Fletcher's capable hands upon me as she brought my children forth from my body and into this world. A little of the turmoil inside me quiets.

William sleeps then, but my mind insists on dwelling upon the thought that even now Mr. Travis must be holding vigil over his father. Though I try to sleep, I hold my own vigil through much of the night.

WILLIAM IS GONE to the burial. I wander out to the garden; it is blustery, the sharp wind promising a coming storm, and I hope that the rain will hold off until the funeral is over even as I rail inwardly at the custom that keeps gently bred women from attending burials. I wrap my arms around myself and walk the gravel paths. My hair, dragged from its pins, whips around my face.

I stop near the lane and look down at the roses. Their leaves rustle, green and gold together, straining in the wind against their stems. I stand for some moments, arms crossed, head bowed, skirt and petticoat twisting around my legs; and then I go inside.

At dinner, William tells me that the funeral was held with

quiet ceremony, attended by the old man's son and nearest male neighbors. My husband speaks highly of his own sermon, which he gives me to read, and which I am sure, as I skim through it, the younger Mr. Travis must have hated. I hand the pages back to William with a few murmured words of praise, then rise early from my place at the table, pleading tiredness.

Chapter Twenty-Two

The maid answers when I knock at the cottage door. Around one arm she wears a black band.

"Is Mr. Travis at home to callers?" I say. My voice is steadier than I expected it would be, given the extent of my apprehension. I spent the walk here reminding myself that it was right and proper for me to visit a bereaved family, but my nerves still buzz, distracting as houseflies, just under my skin. I am torn between a desire to see him, to offer sincere expressions of comfort, and a peculiar sense of fear. I hold myself still, uncertain whether I want the maid's answer to be yes or no.

The other woman nods and beckons me inside with one reddened hand.

She leads me into a long kitchen with a scrubbed wooden table, where Mr. Travis sits mending a harness. He looks up when we enter, and I see surprise in his expression when he notices me.

"Mrs. Parson to see you," the maid says.

Mr. Travis stands and bows. "Mrs. Collins," he says. "Would you—may I offer you some tea, or—"

"No," I say quickly. "That is—thank you, but I—I came to offer my condolences." I raise the basket I am carrying. "I brought you some dinner, as well."

His lips press briefly into a thin line, and then, "Thank you," he says.

I glance at his maid, who steps forward to take the basket from my hands.

When I look back at Mr. Travis, he jerks his hand oddly. "Please," he says, and moves toward the fireplace, in front of which two upholstered chairs are arranged. "Sit down."

I do, and he sits beside me. His maid takes up the broom leaning against the wall and resumes the work she must have abandoned when I arrived, moving to the doorway and sweeping dirt through it with broad, practiced motions. The rasp of the bristles against the floorboards is very loud. My hands grip together, hard. Mr. Travis shifts in his chair, his own hands curled around his knees.

"I was—so very sorry to hear about your father," I say.

"Thank you, Mrs. Collins," Mr. Travis says again. "It is good of you to visit."

"He will be missed," I say, and then I grit my teeth. Our

words are stilted, rote, and though they are the same words I have uttered many times to William's parishioners since I came to Kent, here, now, they feel dreadfully inadequate. I swallow and look away; the maid has leaned her broom up against the wall once more and is walking out the door, a bucket over one arm. I turn back to find Mr. Travis watching me.

"Mr. Travis," I say. "I realize that you must think I am here because it is . . . expected. And of course, it is—that is—I would of course come regardless of . . ." I stop and look down at my fingers, still clasping one another fiercely in my lap. "What I mean to say is that I—when I say that I am sorry, I mean it completely. I regret very deeply that I did not have the opportunity to know your father better, but what I knew of him was . . ." My tongue stumbles, my throat tightens, and I keep my eyes on my hands, struggling for mastery of myself.

"I am sorry for him," I say at last, "and I am sorry for you, and I wish my—my words were not so useless."

There is silence, and then he says, for the third time since my arrival, "Thank you." But this time his voice is rough, and when I gather the courage to look up at him, he is passing a hand across his eyes. Then he looks at me, and a smile, genuine this time, passes like a ghost across his face.

"Do not thank me," I say. "I regret—I wish that I had been able to . . . help somehow."

Another smile, and a small shrug. "There is nothing any-one could have done."

I nod slowly. Looking at him more fully, now, I can see that the skin under his eyes is shadowed; his cheeks are slack. "What happened?" I say.

Mr. Travis shakes his head. "Nothing—nothing. He simply . . . he went to bed as usual, and in the morning, when he was not awake at his usual hour, I tried to rouse him. He would not respond to me, but he was breathing. I went for the doctor, and he . . . Well. He said there was nothing to be done. And I . . . I should have expected this, I suppose. My father was an old man. But it happened very suddenly."

He turns his head away from me so that I cannot see his face, but I can see the muscles of his jaw working. We sit so for a time, I with my hands folded in my lap, he with his shoulders hunched. He is not a tall man—he stands scarcely taller than myself—but he has a physical power formed by hard work. Now, however, in his grief, he looks small. I have an impulse, barely checked, to put my hand upon his.

At last, Mr. Travis draws in a shaky breath. "I apologize," he says, and turns back to me. He looks faintly embarrassed.

"There is no need. I have been lucky—it is hard to imagine the misery of losing a beloved parent."

"Oh, yes." He is rubbing his hands against his thighs. "You were visiting your family—are they all in health?"

"Perfectly. Thank you." I look around the kitchen; it is

largely unornamented, the objects generally of a useful nature, but I spy two coats on pegs beside the door and feel a spasm of sadness, for I recognize the shabbier of the two as old Mr. Travis's. I drag my eyes away, to find his upon me, once more.

"Have you lived with your father all your life?" I say.

He shakes his head. "When he worked for Lady Catherine, he and my mother and I had a cottage on the grounds of Rosings. He and I lived there for some years after my mother died, and then I took on the tenancy here and he lived there alone. It was not until he finally admitted he could not do his work any longer that he came to live here with me."

I glance at the coat, and he follows my gaze, then huffs a soft laugh. "I should give it to Henry Peters—it will be a little large for him, still, but he's a growing lad—but I have not yet been able to . . . That is, it will be strange, not to have it there beside my own." He squints, swallows. "Would you—Mrs. Collins, would it be a terrible imposition to ask you to give it to him? It is—I know it would be easier for me, I see him daily, but—"

"Of course, Mr. Travis," I hasten to say. "Please—think nothing of it. Indeed, you are doing *me* a service—I so often find myself at a loss as to how to help, in such cases as these."

His smile is faint, but it is there, and he opens his mouth as if to speak, only to be interrupted when the maid comes back into the house, her bucket full this time, her gait uneven from the weight of it. She sets it down without looking at us before continuing about her work, going out into the yard once more.

"My father lamented the expense of hiring someone to keep house," Mr. Travis says. His expression is pensive as he looks at the empty doorway. "He was . . . disappointed, that I never married."

There are many things I could say in response, none of which are prudent. "He clearly had the greatest affection for you," I say instead.

"He was a good man." His words are a near echo of his father's, all those weeks ago: *Robby's a good lad.* I blink hard. "My mother died when I was so young—he really had the raising of me."

"He must have been a great deal more . . . present than my father," I say; and then I wince at my own disloyalty. My father has never known quite what to do with any of us; like William, he is a master of the superficial and uncomfortable with anything weightier. I never knew what he thought as I grew older and remained in his house, still unmarried, for he never said a word; I remember his distant smiles, the awkward way he patted my hand. But I also remember the surprising gladness I felt upon his first visit to my new home, the way we clutched one another, the smooth fabric of his waistcoat against my cheek.

Curiosity flickers in Mr. Travis's face, but, politely, he does not ask me to elaborate. There is a little silence, and then he says, "He was . . . present, as you say. But we—I think he resented me, or at least, resented what he saw as his reliance upon me, near the end. And he never tired of needling me about grandchildren." He pushes one hand through his hair, leaving it wilder than before. "And now I wish . . . I feel very selfish, for not giving him that. He would have been a most affectionate grandfather."

We are both, it seems, constantly catching ourselves just at the brink of impoliteness, for I want to ask *why*—why did he never marry, when he is such an amiable man, when he has the means to provide, however modestly, for a family? He is so easy and natural with Louisa—did he never want children of his own?

Mr. Travis's smile is tight, and he is looking at me with a peculiar intensity, as if he guesses my thoughts. I have the distinct feeling that he wants me to voice them. I look back and hold my peace, and at last he says, "How is little Miss Collins? My father—he looked forward to your visits with her. I cannot thank you enough—"

"I wish that I had brought her again sooner after we returned from Hertfordshire," I say in a rush. "Watching them together was such a delight. I meant to come in a day or two—"

I suddenly realize that in my earnestness I have leaned forward across the space between our two chairs. I sit back very quickly.

The maid comes in once more. I have been here for much longer than the customary visiting time. "I am sorry," I say, rising. Mr. Travis looks startled but rises as well. "I have stayed too long—I should not keep you from your work."

"Not at all," he says, but he steps back to allow me to pass before him. We pause at the door; I am hotly aware of the maid's eyes upon us. I look at the coat.

"May I . . . ?"

"Oh—yes." He takes it from its peg, folds it gently in half, holds it pressed for a moment between his hands. His thumb strokes the worn fabric once. "Thank you, Mrs. Collins. Very much." He hesitates, but whatever he might say is forestalled by the maid, edging past us with murmured apologies. I step back to let her pass, and when I look at Mr. Travis, I can see that he will not speak again.

He holds out the coat, and I take it.

I LOOK, BUT the boy Henry is nowhere about as I leave the farm. I will have to bring the coat to him another time, and just as well; it is an easy excuse to call again. The thought makes me shake my head; I open my mouth and begin to sing a song Maria used to practice often. My voice is off-key, but when my muddled thoughts persist in intruding, I sing more loudly. There is no one around to hear.

At home, I set the coat down beside my worktable, for there are loose threads that should be tied off before it is given away. I brush my fingers along the fabric—warm and roughly woven, worn to shiny smoothness at the elbows—then step back. My breathing is slow and regular in my ears, but inside I am unsteady. I want—something. I lick my lips and look out the parlor window.

And blink, as William ambles past. He is muttering to himself, likely practicing his next sermon. I watch him round a bend in the path. My breath, which caught at the back of my throat at the sight of him, releases in a sigh.

Chapter Twenty-Three

There is a packet of handkerchiefs sitting on the desk in William's book room. I saw them once before when William and I were newly wed and, as now, I needed to resupply my writing desk with fresh paper. But then they were tucked away in a drawer. When I asked William about them he replied, "My mother made them."

He did not add anything else, and I was not yet sure enough in our new alliance to pry further.

I touch the faded blue ribbon binding the packet together, trace the intricately worked flowers embroidered along the edge of the handkerchief at the top of the pile. William's mother was skilled with a needle.

I draw my hand back, unexpectedly near tears.

WILLIAM JOINS ME in my parlor after dinner. We sit together near the fire, I with a gown I am letting out for Louisa and he with a letter from Mr. Bennet, one that I know must be in answer to a letter William wrote him long before we journeyed to Hertfordshire.

"William," I say, and wait until he has marked his place with a careful fingertip and looked up at me inquiringly. I return my own eyes to my work and say, striving for a diffident tone, "What exactly was the nature of your father's disagreement with Mr. Bennet?"

There is a pause; I can easily imagine the surprise in his countenance, the wrinkle in his brow. "I never knew," he says at last. "My father was always . . . vociferous in pronouncing his dislike of his cousin, but as to why . . ." Another pause. "Why do you ask, my dear?"

It should not be so difficult to speak of such things, and yet my tongue is clumsy in my mouth and my neck feels hot. "I visited Mr. Travis after his father's funeral. He was just so—very sad. And I realized that we have never spoken of your parents very much."

I cast a quick look at him; William appears as uncomfortable as I feel.

"He—died not long before you came to Kent?" I say.

"Yes." William licks his lips. The hand holding the letter from Mr. Bennet drops slowly until the pages rest against his thighs. "I was pleased that he lived long enough to know about my new position. It is quite a step up in the world from where he began." His glance in my direction is quick, almost furtive. "He was a grocer."

Until now, I have had only the vaguest notion of William's father's circumstances, for they are not something William seems to enjoy discussing. Lizzy once mentioned that her father called his cousin illiterate, but whether that was the literal truth or merely Mr. Bennet's way of sneering at the elder Mr. Collins's way of expressing himself, I do not know. Though I have often wondered whether William's preoccupation with the grandeur of Rosings Park has anything to do with his own parents' humble beginnings.

"I am sure that he was very proud of you," I venture, though in fact I am sure of no such thing.

"I think he must have been," William says, and then, with a little more strength, "Yes, he must have been immensely proud."

I nod, smile, and return my attention to my work. When he speaks, it takes me by surprise.

"My father was a—an excellent man. He gave me every advantage he did not have himself."

I look up, needle poised. "Indeed?"

"Yes." He stands and takes up the poker, prodding at the fire, though it is already burning cheerfully. "He required the utmost respect, as was his right. His authority was absolute. But he always pushed me hard, for he knew my worth.

He knew I, as the inheritor of Longbourn, needed to be ready to take my place among the higher echelons of society." He sets the poker down, returns to his chair. His fingers steeple. "His harshness, I think, was really meant most affectionately. When I spoke to him with the deference he demanded, he was truly very affectionate." He sighs. "If he could have but *seen* me dining with Lady Catherine de Bourgh herself . . . but my comfort is that at least he knew of my new position before I lost him."

If harshness equates to affection in my husband's mind, then his adoration of Lady Catherine suddenly seems at once more understandable and more pitiful. I shift nearer the fire, feeling suddenly cold.

"And your mother?" I say after a pause. "Were she and your father very like?"

William is quiet for so long that I think he has not heard me. But then, "My good mother was gentleness itself," he says.

THE WIND IS brisk, the sky a hazy gray. My fingers clench tightly around the two small bouquets of pinks I cut this morning. They were the last clinging blooms of the season, most of their brethren beginning to wilt and drop their petals; but these still smell rich and spicy, like the cakes I imagined serving my son when he was old enough to enjoy them.

I left Louisa in Martha's care and exited the house for my yearly walk to the churchyard, a solitary tradition that I always look forward to and dread in equal measure. I passed William on my way out of the gate; his smile was pained when I told him where I was going, his eyes quickly sliding away from mine, and I wanted to strike him.

My breath comes in erratic bursts. I avoid the churchyard throughout the rest of the year, for it would be impractical to regularly allow myself to become so completely undone. But now I walk quickly, my strides so long that I must hold the hem of my gown up with the hand not clutching the flowers. I have met no one along the way, for which I am dimly grateful.

MY FIRST BABE was born silently into the world. I was exhausted—dazed—and it took a moment for me to realize that it had been born at all, that the crushing struggle of the past day was over. I felt something brush against my thighs but heard no cry, and for a moment I was confused, could not understand what I was feeling, what I was not hearing. Then the midwife was holding something, something red and damp with limbs that twitched, and was rubbing it, thumping its back, and everything seemed to be happening at a great distance. I had to make myself think, *That is my child.*

At last it gave a cry, so faint I thought I had imagined it. "A boy," said my mother, who had come to Hunsford to be with me during my first confinement. Her expression was

twisted, strange, but my arms reached out of their own voli-
tion, and the midwife, with a glance at my mother, leaned
forward to relinquish him. The navel string dragged across
my softened belly.

I understood my mother's expression as soon as my arms
closed around him. He was weightless, so small it was as
if I held nothing at all. His eyes were tightly closed; when
I touched his hand, his fingers shivered but did not close
around my own. That first cry was more of a gasp, and now I
had to stare at him, hard, to know whether or not he was still
breathing. I stared and stared, watched the faint up-down
movement of his belly, still joined to me by the thick string
that stretched between us.

"Charlotte," my mother said, her voice full of all the things
my mind refused to acknowledge. The breath I did not realize I was holding released, and it sounded as if I were choking. My entire body shook, perhaps from the shock of the
birth, perhaps from the terrible knowledge flooding through
me. "Charlotte, I am going to fetch Mr. Collins."

"No," I said, the word knife-sharp. I touched my baby's
hair—it was dark, as dark as mine, and there was so much
of it that it looked very strange on so small a person, as if he
were wearing a poorly made wig. His chin was mine as well,
distinctly pointed. My breathing was ragged. "No, not yet."

"I must—"

"*No.*" The babe curled against my breast. There were bloody smears on the front of my shift. Though my thoughts skittered, there and gone before I could grasp them, this one thing I knew—William could not see this. I could not share this with him.

"Charlotte," my mother said again, bending over me, brushing my damp hair back from my temples. "My dear girl—please—he must be baptized." I stared at her—I could not comprehend what she was saying—and she put a hand upon each of my shoulders and looked into my face. "He must be baptized *now*," she said, and something inside me splintered. My mother squeezed my shoulders gently before leaving the room.

The midwife said something in my ear, but my body was already curling forward on its own. The afterbirth emerged; she tied off the navel string; I was severed from my son. I stroked his head, pressed my nose to his hair as she moved about the room. I did not know what she was doing, and I did not care.

When my mother reappeared with William, I could not look at either of them. I could only watch my babe's belly rising, falling. Rising again. There was too much space between each breath, and my own breath felt trapped inside my chest. My mother murmured something, and William came forward, his tread heavy. I could see him at the edges of my vision, his hand reaching out only to retreat once more.

"What—" he said, but broke off. I jerked my head to look

at him, and he licked his lips; he was very pale, and his eyes flicked from my face, to the babe, to the pile of bloodstained linens in the midwife's hands. "My dear—what—what is he called?"

He looked so very lost, and I had the dim, faraway feeling that I might, under other circumstances, feel very sorry for him, for William was not made for moments like this. I held my child closer; I would not give him up, not even to his father. Poor William would never hold him. I felt as though someone had plugged my throat and chest with wool; I touched the baby's hair, his pointed chin.

In. Out.

"Lucas," I said, though it sounded like someone else's voice, someone deeply unfamiliar. "Just as we planned, he is called Lucas." I did not look up again. I could not stand it.

Instead, I remained very still and held my son, and did not look at anybody else. A few moments later, William touched my hand where it was cupped against the back of the baby's head, and I started away from him. "I am going to begin," he said. I said nothing, only nodded and stared down at the tiny person in my arms, who stirred briefly at the trickle of water.

"We thank you, Father, for the water of baptism. In it we are buried with Christ in his death . . ."

I felt the catch and hold of my own breathing in too-slow time with my son's. I was lightheaded with lack of air; my eyes burned, desperate to blink.

"Lucas, I baptize you in the name of the Father, and of the Son, and of the Holy Spirit. Amen."

From somewhere behind William, my mother murmured an echoing *amen,* but my own lips were incapable of forming the word.

"Heavenly Father, we thank you that by water and the Holy Spirit you have bestowed upon this your servant the forgiveness of sin . . ."

I cannot breathe, I cannot breathe, I cannot breathe . . .

". . . Give him an inquiring and discerning heart, the courage and will to persevere, a spirit to know and to love you . . ."

Shallow rise of his fragile belly. The brush of William's shaking fingers across a wrinkled forehead, sketching the sign of the cross.

"Lucas, you are sealed by the Holy Spirit in baptism and marked as Christ's own forever."

A howling rising up from my belly; I clamped my lips together to keep it inside, but it emerged, raw and strangled, in bits and pieces.

THE CHURCHYARD IS shaded and silent. Some of the markers are so old they have begun to list to one side or sink deeply into the soil; others, like the one I seek, are only just beginning to weather. I reach it and set one of the bouquets aside, then kneel to place the other upon the earth. I tug at the fingers of my gloves until my hands are free and stretch out my arms to touch the stone. It is small, rough under my fingertips, engraved with only his name, Lucas Collins, and a single date.

I did not see him buried. I listened to the knell of the church bell from my bed and clutched at a pillow with arms that longed instead to hold my child.

I remain kneeling for long minutes, grateful for the quiet, for the solitude. I never know what to think, or what to say; my prayers are half-formed, catching in my throat. As a clergyman's wife, surely I should be capable of praying properly for my child.

My fingers trail across the top of the marker as I rise. My face is wet. I gather the second bouquet and turn, wiping my cheeks with the back of my hand. But I am not alone; there is someone standing beside a grave on the far side of the churchyard, hat off, dark head bowed—Mr. Travis. He must have entered the churchyard while I knelt, unhearing, with my own amorphous thoughts. I am startled enough by his presence, and uncertain enough how to proceed, that I do nothing but stand and stare until it seems he must feel my gaze as a physical touch. He turns, very slowly, and nods to me, clearly unsurprised. I realize that I still have one hand to my cheek; I let it drop to my side and brush my damp palm against the side of my skirt. Then he is moving, and so am I. We walk toward one another through the quiet.

"Mr. Travis," I say. We have stopped under the spreading

branches of an enormous oak tree, and we stand so near one another that I scarcely have to lift my voice at all to be heard. "I did not expect to see you here."

A stupid thing to say, even if it is true. He smiles faintly. "Nor I you. But I have come here most days, since my father . . ."

I look down at the bouquet I am still holding. "I—these are for your father. For his . . ." I tilt my head in the direction from which Mr. Travis has come.

Mr. Travis's jaw hangs loose; he looks at the flowers in my hand and then at my face. "That is very good of you," he says at last. His voice is hoarse.

"No," I say, too sharply. "It is the very, very least I could do." I should have gone instantly to the Travis farm upon returning from Hertfordshire—it was pure cowardice that kept me away, and now old Mr. Travis is gone. He will never see Louisa again—Louisa will never see *him* again, will never again have his pure focused adoration. Guilt presses, and I turn my face away.

There is a little silence, and then he says, "You have nothing with which to reproach yourself."

There are more tears falling over my cheeks. "I do," I say. "I do—"

He makes an abortive motion with one arm, then clasps the back of his neck. I am cloaked in shame and humiliation, but I am helpless to keep from crying. I hold my sobs behind my teeth and squeeze my eyes closed, hugging my elbows and folding forward.

It takes long minutes to calm myself, and my breathing is still ragged when I look back at the place where Mr. Travis was standing. He is still there, though I half-expected that he would, at the very least, retreat to his father's graveside. His brows draw together, but his mouth attempts a smile. "Come," he says, and gestures toward his father's grave. Then he pauses. "Unless you would prefer to offer the flowers in private?"

"No," I say, and he nods, and we cross the churchyard together. The wind is growing stronger, the branches above our heads creaking. His father's grave is indicated not by a stone but by a wooden cross, carved with his name. The earth here still looks freshly disturbed. I lay the flowers at the foot of the cross and stand back, hands folded, again unsure of myself.

"He was a lovely man," I say at last.

Mr. Travis half-smiles. "He certainly could be."

Another cross, weathered and gray, stands nearby. "Your mother?" I say, reading the name.

He nods. "I should make her another marker. It has been too long since I replaced it." He looks back across the church-yard to where my other bouquet rests, incongruously pink and bright in the gathering darkness. "I saw you when I came in," he says, and in his voice is a question. "But I did not want to intrude."

I follow his gaze. "That is—my son," I say.

"A son? I am . . . I should have remembered."

My eyes remain fixed on the flowers marking his grave. "These things are common enough. And we were not . . . so well acquainted, then."

"How long—how long did you have with him?"

I swallow. "Minutes."

I have not truly spoken of my son since his death. My mother is not one to discuss broken hearts, and though she cared for me as I convalesced, she thought it best to parry my need to talk about my babe with happy thoughts about the other children I would surely bear. After the burial, William came up to our room and sat with me for a moment, but he was clearly ill at ease, and we have not spoken of our first child since except for these visits, which I always mention, and which always seem to make him uncomfortable. He hovered ceaselessly, though, hovered until I longed to scream, when I was increasing with Louisa—he had been solicitous of my comfort when I carried our firstborn, but it was nothing to this. He invaded my parlor, insisted that I not walk anywhere farther from the parsonage than Rosings Park, monitored what I ate and drank, and asked Lady Catherine for advice, which she was all too happy to give, about the healthfulness of this or that food or tonic. His anxiety might have been more bearable had my own not been so high, and as we never discussed the seat of our mutual fear,

I could not feel the sweetness behind his attentions, only the irritation they inspired.

"He was too small—so very, very small," I say now, and it is as if the words have been locked away inside of me for years, just waiting for the moment they would be allowed to burst forth. "I don't know why. He was not very early, only a little, but . . ." The midwife had said it happens like that, sometimes, a babe born scrawny and sickly, as if it had been confined too tightly inside the womb. I take several steps away from Mr. Travis and press my hand against the thick raised bark of a tree to anchor myself, for I am suddenly too light, floatable. "And he was beautiful. I *know* that, I remember that, but I cannot—I wish I could still see him clearly. I wish . . ."

He approaches. "I know," he says, soft. "I cannot remember my mother, really. Not the details of her. But the essentials—those remain."

"Yes," I gasp out, and blink up at the treetops to ward away still more tears. The air has grown suddenly wet and heavy, thick with water droplets that do not so much fall as hang, mist-like, around us. I should return home before the rain begins in earnest, but I do not move. "Thank you—thank you for speaking with me. I appreciate it. Very much." It is only with great restraint that I keep from fidgeting.

Mr. Travis looks down at me, inscrutable. "I always enjoy speaking with you," he says.

The wind buffets me, and I shiver. "And I you."

A heartbeat later: "What was he called?"

I exhale a short, stunned breath. Gratitude blooms behind my breastbone.

"Lucas," I say. "His name was Lucas."

I AM WITHIN sight of the parsonage when the rain suddenly begins falling heavily. Running, I make it inside the gate and under the eaves near the door, but here I stop and look out over the garden. Through the rain everything is hazy, and I am profoundly tired in a way that has nothing to do with physical exertion. I lean back against the wall of the house and breathe deeply of the wet air.

Inside the house, William is no doubt in his book room. Over dinner, in a few hours, we will eat and drink together and make conversation. I will ask whether Miss de Bourgh went for a ride in her phaeton despite the threatening weather. He will say she did not. He will not ask about my visit to the churchyard. I will resent him for it.

But something taps at my mind. When William spoke of his father, his words left me with a profound sense of sadness. I know he must feel affection toward Louisa, but it is rare that he manages to show it; perhaps it should not surprise me that he does not know how to express his grief over the son we lost. Perhaps, I think, he sits home on this day each year, remembering alone, while I make my annual walk to the churchyard. Perhaps he remembers our child's face with increasing blurriness, as I do; perhaps he wakes sometimes with the sensation that, in his sleep, he recalled Lucas's features with painful, perfect clarity.

Or perhaps he does not think about our firstborn at all.

I push away from the wall and stand under the very edge of the eave, watching the rain fall like a curtain just a breath away from me. I cannot believe that William is so coldhearted, not when I have seen the evidence of his natural feelings myself in his mother's handkerchiefs, so long cherished.

The rain drums on the gravel pathways. I am growing cold, but I cannot seem to make myself move from this spot.

There is lavender drying in the stillroom. Its fragrance would be a lovely surprise for William to discover one day, a few sprigs tucked in among the handkerchiefs. The thought brings only a little pleasure, contrasted as it is with the thought of tonight's meal and the hours after, which stretch colorlessly before me.

I wish the rain had kept away longer, that I might have conversed with Mr. Travis just a few minutes more.

I turn and go into the house.

have spent the last hour kneeling among the raspber-ries. There are streaks of dirt on my apron and long scratches on the backs of my hands, but I am finally satisfied that I have gathered all the berries I can find.

I sit so for several minutes, then sigh and push myself up off the ground. Lifting my basket, I start back toward the house. There are enough berries to make up small packets for at least five families, and this I set to doing quickly once inside the kitchen, folding handfuls of raspberries into squares of cloth and tying them with snips of twine, then settling each packet into the bottom of the basket. Upstairs, I hear the sound of laughter and running feet as Louisa eludes Martha, and then Mrs. Baxter's startled shout as they, presumably, hurtle toward her. I smile. William was summoned to Rosings this morning, and it seems to me that we are all taking advantage of his absence.

The packets made up, I go to my parlor to retrieve old Mr. Travis's coat, now carefully mended. This I place, folded, atop the basket's other contents. Then I tie a bonnet over my hair but forgo my spencer. I feel distinctly girlish as I step into the lane, the ribbon on my bonnet blowing back from my face, the autumn sun weak but still offering a little lovely, residual warmth.

I make my way from one tenant's home to another, giving three of the berry packets to large families. The fourth I bring to Mrs. Fitzgibbon, who is as delighted by the treat as any of the children.

And now, at last, I turn my feet toward the Travis farm.

I should have come earlier—I mended the coat within a day of receiving it—but I have been slow to gather my courage. The most prudent course would be to leave the coat at the Peterses' cottage, for I know young Henry must go home to his parents on Sundays, but I have not been able to bring myself to squander the excuse to visit the Travis farm. Acknowledging this makes me flush, but my steps as I climb the hill toward the farm are firm.

I arrive to find Henry Peters engaged in mending a fence. I hold out the coat and explain its origins, and he takes it from me, stammering his thanks. When I depart, I look back over my shoulder to see that he has folded the coat very carefully over a rail on an unbroken section of fence before returning to his labor.

I am nearly to the cottage, intending to leave the berries with the maid, when I see Mr. Travis emerge from an outbuilding, and it is the most natural thing in the world to smile and settle with him against a crumbling stone wall. We are sheltered, here, from view from the house, but if anyone else were to happen by we are still perfectly, respectably in view of the surrounding fields. There is a small pause; we are both looking down at the berries I have brought, which tumbled from their neat pile when I untied their wrappings.

"Have a berry, Mr. Travis," I finally say.

He smiles, reaches out. His hands are filthy, which he seems to realize at the same time as I do; his hand hovers in midair, and then, with surprising delicacy, he plucks a single berry from the top of the pile, so carefully that he touches only the one. I take one as well, and we chew for a moment in silence. I look at him, and then away, across the shorn fields.

"I gave your father's coat to Henry Peters," I say. "He handled it with such care, I believe it must mean a great deal to him."

"Thank you. I am . . . embarrassed by my own cowardice. I should have delivered the coat myself."

"Please," I say, and turn back to look at him, reaching out my hand. It hangs in the air between us until I drop it once more to my side. "I cannot imagine it would be easy to give up a—a tangible reminder of the person you lost. It is to your credit that you were generous enough to part with it at all."

He is silent for a long moment before finally saying, "My father was very . . . unsettled in the days before he died." He is holding another berry between his thumb and forefinger, and in his hand it looks comically small. "He snapped at me, he snapped at Betsy—our maid—so much that I was afraid the poor girl would start looking for a new position. Neither of us could do anything to please him."

"Perhaps he was not feeling . . . entirely himself."

"I wonder whether he knew." Mr. Travis shakes his head. "I do not see how he could, of course, but—I wonder. He was so unlike himself, I wonder whether he somehow—knew—that he had little time left. He spent much of his last day in the garden—kept me for hours from my own work, pruning and trimming things to his standards." He rubs his free hand over his jaw. "I cannot help but think he knew. And he must have realized I would not have the time to keep the garden up as he would like. And while Betsy keeps the vegetables tolerably well, she knows nothing of other plants."

It is the second time Mr. Travis has mentioned the maid in as many minutes, and it puts me in mind of his observation that old Mr. Travis had wished his son had no need to hire a maid at all.

"Did you never have the inclination to marry?" I say, then immediately want to cut out my tongue, which has moved so much quicker than thought or good sense. I am not speaking to Elizabeth or Maria, no matter how naturally Mr. Travis and I might converse; I cannot assume the liberties I am accustomed to with my friend and my sister.

If Mr. Travis is offended by my poor manners, he does not show it. Instead, he looks down at the berry he holds. "No," he says. "I never did." He looks up at me. "That is, I suppose I've been inclined toward marriage in a general way, but never with a view toward a specific woman. There are few enough options in Hunsford."

This is certainly true. When you are born into small country-village society, limited marriage prospects are to be expected—Lizzy and I joked about Meryton's shallow pool of eligible men often enough. When rich, unwed Mr. Bingley arrived in the neighborhood the same year I met William, it caused a tremendous fluttering among the village's mammas. Their excited scheming would have been funny had it not been rooted in such reasonable anxiety about their daughters' futures. And Mr. Travis lives in Hunsford, which is smaller even than the village of my girlhood—he has never left Kent at all, never had any opportunity to meet anyone outside the circle into which he was born.

I remember the murmured rush through the congregation when Miss Harmon first arrived. A young, pretty woman, suddenly coming into a community full of unwed and widowed men; it is a wonder, I think now, that she has not received multiple offers of marriage already. But thinking of Miss Harmon makes me feel suddenly cross, and to distract myself I put a berry between my teeth. It bursts sweet and sour against my tongue, tasting of summer in the same way the pale sun feels like it, a last, generous gasp. When I have swallowed I say, "Not everyone has the luxury of waiting until love comes along. I think I told you my sister married for love, but what if she had not met Mr. Cowper when she did? She would have had no choice but to marry someone else, someone who could offer her comfort. She does not have a farm to work, as you do."

He looks amused. "Would you wish a farm for her, if she had not found love?"

My mouth opens, then closes again. I look up at the sky, spreading wide and bright above us. Now they have been spoken, my words seem nonsensical. "No," I say, because it is the sensible thing. "Of course not. And I—well, Maria thinks I lack the soul for poetry. I suppose I should not speak of things I do not fully understand."

"I do not care for poetry. But I do not see what poetry has to do with . . . I imagine a man can not read poetry, and yet still find love."

I stare. "But—you have never been in love."

His mouth twists a little at the corners. "I did not say that."

I am the first to drop my eyes. After a moment, from the edges of my vision, I see him take another berry. I listen to him chew and swallow. He says, "Mr. Collins has asked me to come look at the parsonage roses."

Startled, I say, "When did he have a chance to do that?" Mr. Travis did not attend church last Sunday; perhaps he and William met in the village.

Mr. Travis winces. "After he finished my father's service."

Shock holds me fast. William can be thoughtless, yes, but to importune a man mere moments after his father was laid to rest . . .

"I am very sorry," I say, but Mr. Travis shakes his head.

"I should not have mentioned it. And Mr. Collins did apologize for the insensitivity of his timing, but he said the roses are in such a bad way that he feared delaying his request might be disastrous. I only spoke of it because I hoped you would tell Mr. Collins that I intend to come tomorrow morning, and to apologize to him for the delay."

He is smiling, a little. I find that I cannot. "Mr. Travis, you need not apologize."

"Well. I hope . . . if you happen to be in when I call, I would appreciate your, er, opinion of the roses' condition. I fear Mr. Collins was so distraught that I could not understand how long they have been suffering."

There is a slight breeze; it stirs his hair. I glance away. He knows I've no knowledge of gardening. "Yes, I will be home."

"Ah. Good."

For want of something to do, I take another raspberry. He says, with a casual air, "What of you?"

I am startled into looking at him. "What do you mean?"

There is a strange, defiant sort of bravado in his face. It turns him into someone unfamiliar. "Would you have rather had a farm, Mrs. Collins?"

"I—"

But Mr. Travis presses his fingertips to the bridge of his nose. When he looks at me again, it is with a mortified expression. "I beg your pardon," he says. "That was—horribly rude."

His embarrassment calms me. "I do not know," I say. Mr. Travis stares at me, and I smile a little. "That is to say, I cannot truly say yes, for had I not married, there would be no Louisa, and that is . . . unimaginable. Yet I think—were such a choice available to me, were marriage not the only way I could find . . . Yes, I think I might have chosen to run a little farm."

"Indeed?"

I am smiling foolishly. "I think I would, yes." But this is too disloyal. I think of poor William and am suddenly ashamed of myself.

Mr. Travis leans nearer, peering at my face. "Please," he says, "do not distress yourself. It was I who asked the question—my impertinence was unpardonable."

My laugh is a short, empty thing. "I should not have answered, and certainly not as I did."

"Perhaps not, but . . ."

I lean back against the wall and cross my arms. "My friend Elizabeth—Mrs. Darcy—could not understand my decision to marry as I did. To accept security. And comfort." I squint into the distance. "Rather than love."

Mr. Travis is quiet for a time, but I can feel his eyes upon me. "I think it a shame," he says finally, "that your friend could not recognize the courage it must have taken for you to leave everything you loved and start again somewhere new. You have brothers?"

I nod but cannot trust myself to look at him.

"Well, then you could have remained somewhere familiar, and still, presumably, lived out your life in some comfort."

"I could not have," I say, and push away from the wall. "That is, I *could* have, but it would have been—to be such a burden, to know I was *always* going to be such a burden, and then to have the possibility of my own life, my own home, offered to me by—by a good man, a—respectable man . . ."

"Please forgive me," Mr. Travis says again, very softly, and steps away from the support of the wall as well. He looks flustered, brushing his fingertips along the edges of his coat before lifting down the basket and holding it out like an offering.

"The last raspberry of the season is yours," he says.

I take it.

Chapter Twenty-Five

Walking home, I have the most peculiar urge to strip my feet bare of their half boots and stockings and feel them firm against the earth. And then, perhaps, to press my entire self against the ground, to inhale and fill my lungs and tether myself with the smells of tree roots and undergrowth and the fresh dampness of decaying matter. I even stop walking, just for a moment, breathe in and out, flex my fingers against the handle of the basket to keep them from flying to my bootlaces. When I begin moving again, it is with the sense that my strange compulsion is dragging at me, and so I step more quickly, lifting my feet higher to leave it behind.

AROUND MIDNIGHT, THERE is a crashing storm.

I have been lying sleepless for hours, and at the first flash of lightning I am out of bed and across the room. I lean close to the window and peer outside, but though I can hear the wind rising, all is darkness. The clap of thunder that follows makes me jump; I look over my shoulder, but William appears to be sleeping on. Then the heavens release the rain—it pelts down over the window, and I imagine it pooling in the garden below, running in rivulets down the lane. Turning Mr. Travis's fields to mud. I lean my forehead against the glass.

I have never been friends with a man before. I did not think such a thing was possible, really. Friendship between women is entirely natural—we live in the same world, we share the same concerns. But men. Men have always seemed a species apart; even my father and my brothers, though beloved, are not creatures I truly understand, nor, if I am honest, ever really cared to.

Would you have rather had a farm, Mrs. Collins?

It was easy to say yes to Mr. Travis's question now, when I have the comfortable life of a prosperous clergyman's wife. I press my face into my palms, embarrassment making my cheeks hot. What do I know of running a farm?

And yet . . .

I let my hands drop, palms trailing down my cheeks, my throat, my breasts. They brush my hips and thighs. And I suddenly wish, with an unfamiliar clench in the deepest part of my belly, that *he* would touch me there, and there, and there—and that I could touch him. I could run my fingers over the roughness of his cheeks, through the softness of his hair, against the callused palms of his hands. I have never felt such a compulsion, and for a moment I am ashamed—if I must harbor such thoughts, they should be for the man who lies sleeping in the bed behind me. For the first time, I have some small understanding of what it is that makes girls like Lydia Bennet run off with men who can offer them nothing but pretty words.

Today, Mr. Travis and I were both impolite. I drop my hands and look over at William. With him, I look forward to a lifetime of politeness. Just for a moment, I have a heady thought—if only I had waited to marry, just for a few years more. If I had waited until—

My hands clench into fists. What *utter* foolishness. If I had not married William, I would be living still in Meryton with my parents. I would be an old maid. There would be no Louisa and no prospect of future children. And, of course, I would not have met Mr. Travis. I would be sitting in my mother's parlor and he would be tending his farm, each of us utterly ignorant of the other's existence.

And besides, I would not have married a farmer. I was too sensible for that.

I return to my bed. William has rolled in his sleep toward the center of the mattress, so I fit myself carefully against him in the space left for me.

Chapter Twenty-Six

The sky has been dark with clouds since I awoke, so dark that it hardly feels as if there was a dawn at all. Martha and Louisa are in the nursery and William is in his book room. I have been sitting in my parlor for several hours, sewing clothing for the cottagers and looking up at the window every other minute to see whether Mr. Travis has arrived in the garden, or if the clouds have opened, dropping rain as they have been threatening to do, so that he cannot come at all. My foot moves in restless time with the ticking of the mantel clock. I have the disconcerting idea that this must be what it is like to sit home awaiting a call from a suitor; this thought, like so many I have had of late, leaves me flustered.

Mrs. Baxter enters with the post, and I accept it, grateful for the distraction. A letter from my mother, the direction written clearly in her careful, looped hand.

The page is filled with the usual news of home and the gossip from the most recent card party at the Phillipses'. As I read I pull my legs up and settle more deeply into my chair.

And then, this: *Mrs. Bennet tells me her husband is recovering nicely from the cough he developed just after Maria's wedding. But then, I imagine she has reason to be less open in her speech with me than she might once have been. In any event, Mr. Bennet has not been to church in two weeks.*

My mother's tone is restrained, but I imagine her half smile, the eagerness in her expression as she penned those sentences. I read through quickly to the letter's closing, then set it down on the table beside me.

There are voices out in the garden. I glance at the window, but there is no one in sight; a moment of straining to listen and I determine that the voices are decidedly masculine. I look at the letter but do not pick it up; I cannot think what to say to my mother just yet. I look at the window but do not move to go outside. The voices fade, the speakers moving farther away from the house, perhaps, and inside my head my mother's voice says, *Mr. Bennet has not been to church in two weeks;* and I am alarmingly numb.

Then something inside of me gives a hard jerk, and I am suddenly up, opening the parlor door and rushing down the hallway until, somehow, I find myself in the garden. The wind is strong enough that it precludes any chance of hearing voices more than a few steps away, but I make my way toward the front gate, head bowed and arms folded across my ribs for warmth.

They are standing before the roses, Mr. Travis and my husband. William has one hand pressed flat to the top of his head in an attempt to keep his hat in place; Mr. Travis has abandoned his hat altogether, and his hair blows comically about his head like tall grasses in a meadow. He is gesturing at the roses, but I cannot hear his words, the wind snatching them away before they can reach me, and William is turned away from me. I can feel the wind tearing at my hair, wrapping my skirt around my legs. I should feel ridiculous, out of doors without so much as a shawl, but Mr. Travis looks up and sees me. He stops talking and looks, just for the smallest moment—his mouth smiles, and his eyes, and I smile back. Then William says something and Mr. Travis turns his attention back to him.

My skin is growing pebbled from the cold air, so I turn and walk away, suddenly hoping very much that William will not turn around. I do not want to hear his questions, or the inevitable scolding over my inadequate attire. I look back once; Mr. Travis seems absorbed by whatever William is saying, but he glances up at me, again just for a moment, and nods.

"I . . . HEARD YOU speaking with Mr. Travis," I say to William. We stand together in the entranceway, my back turned to him as he helps me on with my wrap. We are invited to a

card party at Rosings Park, which William has been anticipating with pleasure for days. Colonel Fitzwilliam, another
of Lady Catherine's nephews, will be there, along with the
lady to whom he has recently become engaged; my husband
has been in a froth of curiosity ever since Lady Catherine
mentioned the engagement a fortnight ago.

William's fingers still upon my shoulders. "Why, yes," he
says. "Mr. Travis did come today."

There is something odd about his voice. "Is anything the
matter?"

"No—no," he says, and turns away to find his hat, but not
before I have seen the redness of his complexion. "I wanted
him to look at the roses and . . . he says the yellowing leaves
are the result of overwatering."

I am puzzled. "That is a good thing, is it not? It is something you can correct?"

"Yes, it is. But I am *mortified* that I have inadvertently
caused such harm."

I place a hand on his forearm. "You did the right thing in
asking for advice," I say. "I am only sorry that I discouraged
you from doing so."

His smile is indulgent. "You are always very good, trying
not to trouble anyone, but you had not the understanding of
what was required in this instance, which is why I did not
concern myself overmuch with your opinion."

MISS WATTERS, COLONEL Fitzwilliam's bride-to-be, accepts my congratulations on her engagement with a smile that is chilly as rainwater. She is gowned in silk, her bandeau adorned with curled and dyed ostrich feathers. Her brother, also impeccably dressed and groomed, is polite but distant, his eyes on the brandy in his glass. Colonel Fitzwilliam, by contrast, seems genuinely happy to meet us again; he asks after our daughter and about the Darcys' recent visit with every appearance of true interest.

William is soon drawn to Lady Catherine's side by her command, and Mr. and Miss Watters drift away. The colonel watches them go with an abstracted expression, his eyes, unusually cold, on the sweep of Miss Watters's gown as she walks.

"How did you and Miss Watters become acquainted?" I say, and he turns his attention back to me with a smile.

"We were introduced at a ball in London. It was her first Season; I was, ah . . . fortunate enough to win her affection."

The colonel steps closer. "My aunt insisted upon meeting Miss Watters as soon as I wrote to her of the engagement. What do you think, Mrs. Collins—does Lady Catherine approve my choice?"

We both glance at Miss Watters, who has now moved to Lady Catherine's side. The tilt of her head, the way she holds her glass, both speak of careful breeding. She is young,

clearly, but does not act it, and when she speaks to her ladyship, she is all smiles and deference.

"I think Miss Watters will do very well," I say.

Colonel Fitzwilliam takes a sip from his glass. "Yes, I think
so, too."

AFTER CARDS, LADY Catherine calls for a light supper, served
informally in the drawing room, and orders Miss Watters to
play for us all. Miss Watters plays and sings two complicated
songs with great exactitude and very little emotion, which
seems to please her ladyship greatly, despite her oft-repeated
criticisms of Mrs. Jenkinson for playing without proper feeling for the music.

Lady Catherine scarcely waits until the final note has
sounded before beginning her interrogation. "Do you draw,
Miss Watters?"

"I do, ma'am," Miss Watters says, and smiles modestly.

"I suppose you had a governess," Lady Catherine says,
looking her over.

"Yes, ma'am."

"She seems to have done her job tolerably well. And your
father made his fortune in manufacturing?" She turns to
look at Mr. Watters, who masks his annoyance with impressive quickness.

"Yes, Your Ladyship." His smile is tight.

Lady Catherine sniffs. "A pity, that, but I suppose it cannot be helped. My nephew hasn't the fortune to attract someone with the right connections." She nods at Colonel Fitzwilliam, who is watching the exchange with narrowed eyes. "I suppose my brother has met her?"

If Miss Watters resents being spoken of as if she were not present, she has the good sense not to show it.

Colonel Fitzwilliam nods. "He has, Aunt." A brief, impersonal smile toward Miss Watters. "He approved heartily."

"He always was too liberal with his approval," Lady Catherine says. "See how quickly he approved Darcy's choice!" But her expression softens, just a little. "*Your* choice, however, Nephew, is worth approving, I think."

The party disperses soon after that, Lady Catherine declaring that it is time for those of us not staying at Rosings to leave. A footman leads us from house to carriage for the short ride back to the parsonage. I am preoccupied; I spent much of the evening watching the colonel and his intended as they played at quadrille with Lady Catherine and Mr. Watters. They scarcely exchanged three words, and Colonel Fitzwilliam's usually affable manner was absent. That the marriage is clearly one of convenience on both sides—he offers her connections to the nobility, she brings him a fortune by way of her substantial dowry—once would not have troubled me at all. That I find it troubling now troubles me even more.

Chapter Twenty-Seven

Today it has been raining without stop, and I have closed myself in my parlor with the fire lit and my chair dragged nearer the window, the better to make use of its pale gray light. I have not answered my mother's letter, and I have not mentioned its contents to William. Instead, I drown out thoughts of what I ought to be doing with the scratch of my pencil against paper, losing myself in line and shadow. The task is restful; I don't have to think, which is exactly what I need right now. There is something comforting in the idea that in this, at least, I can muddle along and, slowly, see small improvements with each attempt.

When at last I raise my head and find that it is already time for tea, I have again discarded more drawings than not. But there are a few—small studies, merely, unpolished and taken entirely from memory—that I think, perhaps, I can eventually turn into something better.

THE AIR IS fresh and cool, the ground still wet, but I am determined to take Louisa for a walk. She has been cooped up in the house for far too long, without even the occasional run around the garden. Her little legs want stretching. And I want—I want—something. To be out of the house. Out of the yard. Away from the letter that still waits for my response in the parlor.

I lace us both into our sturdiest boots and we set out down the lane. Louisa dashes toward every puddle, and despite my best efforts we have not gone far out of sight of the parsonage before her boots, stockings, and hem are filthy. The leaves are starting to turn; I point out the colors as we pass, though I am not sure whether Louisa hears me at all, so intent is she upon dragging a stick through the mud behind her.

We leave the woods behind and head out through the fields. I feel the damp dragging at my skirt and petticoat and lift my hems. My legs are free to stride as they please; I run with my child through the tall grass.

It is Louisa who spots him first, stopping short and raising a finger to point. I look, and there is Mr. Travis, small at this distance but still unmistakable. He lifts his hat; I take Louisa's hand and pull her forward.

"Mrs. Collins, Miss Collins." Mr. Travis smiles, highlighting the lines about his eyes and mouth. "It is a rather damp day for a walk."

"We have been kept inside far too long. Louisa has been going a bit mad."

He reaches out a hand to touch Louisa's round cheek. "She has grown, even since I saw her last."

"I think she has grown since *I* saw her last."

A chuckle, then a pause. "What is your destination?"

"I did not have one in mind." I peer up at him. "And yours?"

His face is so tan that it is difficult to tell, but I think perhaps he is flushing. "I . . . had a mind to check on your roses."

Now it is I who blushes. His smile is rueful. But when I speak, it is with an air of nonchalance. "I take this walk frequently," I say. "I like the . . . solitude. It is rare that we see another person."

He lifts his brows. "Then I suppose I should apologize for intruding on your solitude."

I shake my head. "In your case, there is no intrusion."

He smiles, wide and toothy, and looks away across the field. We both watch Louisa, her dress soaked from hem to knee, as she wanders away from us. I set my mind to the task of finding something mundane to say and settle at last upon, "Mr. Collins tells me the harvest was particularly abundant this year. Lady Catherine is very pleased."

"As are her tenants," Mr. Travis says dryly. "Though there is some concern that such abundance might lead her ladyship to think the time is right to increase rents."

My brows go up. "Indeed? Has she done so in the past?"

"To her credit, generally only in times of plenty, when we can best afford it. Though it does rankle somewhat that we are unable, then, to enjoy increased prosperity ourselves. And it might be that it is Mr. Colt whom we have to thank in such cases; I do not know how deeply involved Lady Catherine herself is in the running of the estate."

"Nor do I, though I would be . . . surprised . . . if Lady Catherine did not take an interest in all aspects of her estate."

We exchange quick smiles and both look away again.

"Well," he says at last. "If rents *are* increased, I fear there will be more parishioners in need of your assistance this winter."

I look at Louisa, who has chosen to sit herself down in the middle of the field, no doubt adding mud and grass stains to the wetness of her skirt. I should scold her but cannot muster the will; instead, my mind has flown back to my parlor and the letter tucked into a cubby in my writing desk.

"There is a chance," I say slowly, "that we will no longer be in Kent this winter."

Speaking the words releases some pressure within me, and I exhale a great breath.

Mr. Travis stands statue-like for a moment, then says, "Why?"

I tell him, haltingly, about my mother's letter. "It could be nothing. Mr. Bennet might be perfectly well at this very moment. But . . . even if he is, he will not live forever. Mr. Collins is heir to the estate; someday, we must leave here."

I've always known this, of course; indeed, when I accepted William's proposal, it was with the glad understanding that our time in Kent would be limited, and that I would someday return to Hertfordshire and be near my family. But it is only now that the reality of my situation is no longer something to anticipate with pleasure. Nothing has changed, not truly, and yet my world is slipping sideways, away from me.

Mr. Travis clears his throat. I look at him, sturdy and wind-blown. He does not smile now, though his eyes are gentle under those wild brows. He bends at the waist, a small bow.

As he rises he says, "Your friends will have to make the most of your company, then, while they still have it."

Chapter Twenty-Eight

When I write at last to my mother, I simply ignore her mention of Mr. Bennet's illness and talk instead of lighter things. To William, I say nothing; there is, after all, no certainty that his cousin will not rally and live for another ten years or more, and I cannot face the eager speculation with which he is almost certain to greet the news.

But as the days slip by like the pages of a book turned too quickly, passing through the bursting color of autumn to the blue-gray of winter, there is an unreal quality about them. I cannot be certain that my time in Kent is limited, but neither can I shake away the feeling that I am living in a suspended moment. Hunsford has become home to me, quite suddenly and without my noticing the change. My confidence has grown, since that first visit to Mrs. Fitzgibbon, and I have begun to call with greater frequency upon the parishioners, not only when I know a baby is due or that someone is ill, but at regular intervals, with little treats for the children and notions for the women that they might enjoy, but on which they would not likely spend their own hard-earned coin. I am fully occupied, and it feels good. If the tenants are surprised by my new attentiveness, they are too polite to say so, and no one seems to find my visits intrusive, as I once feared they would.

And I have a friend, at last, someone whose mind and spirit resonate with my own. Such a difference a single true friend makes. My thoughts and feelings are lighter for having someone with whom I can share them. The leaves change around me, the wind grows bitter, and yet, for the first time since my marriage, I am truly happy. Even knowing, as I think I do, that this new, easy season must soon end.

MR. TRAVIS AND I have met accidentally several times since that day in the damp field; sometimes Louisa is with me, bundled in her cap and spencer, but often she remains with Martha at the parsonage while I take baskets to the cottagers, walking slowly through the fallow fields between Rosings Park and the tenants' farms.

We also see each other in Hunsford more than once, but neither of us ever acknowledges the other beyond the briefest of courtesies—we nod, our eyes catching for only a moment, and then walk on. At church, we do not speak, though it is harder there, when I am not moving, to keep my gaze from lingering upon his face and figure. I do my best to keep my back to him and to not allow myself to be drawn into conversation with those in his vicinity, for surely, surely if we were to stand close together, everyone must feel the intimacy between us?

"I RETURNED THE book you gave me," I tell him today. I have brought my sketching things, and I am trying to draw the view. Mr. Travis sits, knees drawn up to his chest, and watches as I rub out yet another false start.

"I'm glad to hear it," he says. "Though I assumed you had, as no fines were issued on my account." He leans over, takes up one of the drawings I set aside, and turns it this way and that. "Was it useful?"

I smile a little. "If you call encouraging me to waste a great deal of paper *useful* . . ."

"If you enjoy it, then yes, I do." He holds out the paper in his hand. "You are too critical of your own efforts."

I keep my eyes upon my work. "I do enjoy it. But I fear I will never be truly good at it." I set my pencil down and study what I have created so far—bare-branched trees, sloping meadow grasses—and frown.

"I think you've made an excellent start."

"I will begin again another day." But even as I say the words, the knowledge thuds through me, a stone dropped from a great distance: I might have few opportunities remaining to draw this particular view. I should not waste this one.

And then, horribly, I remember: "I drew your father once, Mr. Travis."

The hope in his face makes me want to weep. "You did?"

I can recall it clearly, the half-formed portrait: old Mr. Travis's face, wrinkles spread across it like a delicate root system.

"I'm sorry," I say. My voice is brittle as spring ice. "I regret this—so very much. I cannot remember what left me so dissatisfied with it."

It takes a moment, but Mr. Travis understands my meaning. He looks at me and sighs. His eyes are brown, which should not matter, it should not be something I notice at all. But it does; it is. They are brown, like mine. Like William's, and Louisa's, and those of a hundred other people I have met. A most ordinary thing, brown eyes. His father's eyes were brown, as well. I turn my face aside until I am able to compose myself.

"I never thanked you properly for the book," I say at last. "It was a very thoughtful thing to do."

"It was a very thought*less* thing to do."

"Impertinent, perhaps," I say after a moment, looking sideways at him. "But not thoughtless."

A LETTER FROM Elizabeth contains no mention of her father's health, and at first I take this as a positive sign that he is well. But then I think—would she mention it if he were not? As dear to one another as Lizzy and I are, we have never once discussed that I will someday be mistress of her father's estate, and I suppose she might feel strange if there were reason to acknowledge that "one day" might be coming rather sooner than later.

"WHAT MADE YOU choose this path? Farming, I mean, since you were not raised to it."

Mr. Travis and I sit on a hill a little ways from Rosings's woods. The surrounding fields are still green from the rain, the hedgerows a little darker. On the edges of the fields, the trees weep golden leaves, and the sky is stretched taut above us, bare of clouds.

We have been here for half an hour or more; the chill of the ground is beginning to seep through my pelisse, gown, and petticoat, but at least it is not damp. I do not wish to move. There is something both precious and precarious in these moments, and I hover within them—as I walk out from the parsonage, wondering whether I will meet Mr. Travis coming from the other direction; as we see one another and smile, both of us pretending we have not noticed the new frequency of such meetings; as, without having to consult one another, we find a spot to sit, the niceties utterly unnecessary. In choosing to visit with me, he is sacrificing valuable time on his farm, but the one time I tentatively voiced this concern, he was gruff in his dismissal of it. "It's all right," he said, his tone shorter than it normally was when he spoke to me. "I have time." I thought I understood his terseness, for I had just acknowledged something we had tacitly agreed to leave *un*acknowledged; and so I said nothing more.

Today we crested this hill together, walking so quickly that when we reached the top my breath was coming in great gasps; when I looked at Mr. Travis, I was happy to see that he felt the exertion, as well. He caught my eye, and a slow grin spread across his face. I could feel my own smile answering his, and then suddenly we were laughing, for no reason at all.

"It is not as if there were a great many choices available to me," Mr. Travis says now, slowly. He looks at me sideways. "The son of a gardener cannot afford the education of a gentleman. And I like working in the open air. But—I was not satisfied by the prospect of keeping the gardens at Rosings Park for the rest of my life."

"Indeed? Rosings's gardens are very beautiful." I make my voice neutral and raise my eyes to the pale sky.

He hesitates, then says, "Yes, I would agree, though perhaps mostly out of loyalty to my father, for he is the one who implemented most of Lady Catherine's, ah, improvements. But we have spoken of this before, I think, and I told you then that I am neither artist nor poet." A pause. "But still, beauty comes in many forms, does it not? And I find more of it looking out over a well-tended field than walking among manicured topiaries."

Something in his voice makes my stomach tighten. I look at him sharply, and Mr. Travis returns the look with his usual steadiness. My breath whispers out through parted lips.

"Do you compare me to a field, Mr. Travis?" I might have asked, were I young and unmarried and accustomed to flirtation. But I am none of these things, so I close my mouth over the words that jostle for release behind it.

TODAY, HE STANDS near the churchyard. I am a little ways away, just outside the church door, greeting the last stragglers as they exit the building. He is joined by Mr. and Mrs. Prewitt and their niece, who looks very charming in a wide-brimmed bonnet trimmed with flowers. Mrs. Prewitt, as ever, seems to be doing much of the talking. I make myself look elsewhere.

"What do you think of that?" Mrs. Fitzgibbon says. She has come up beside me, and her eyes, sharp as a crow's, have noticed to where my attention keeps wandering.

I swallow down my instinctive fear at having been observed and say dryly, "I think that Mrs. Prewitt might be playing matchmaker."

Apparently, Mrs. Fitzgibbon wheezes when she laughs too hard.

The little group is still standing there when William and

I are ready to return home. They stop talking when we pass, murmuring their good-byes. Mr. Travis's eyes flicker toward my hand upon William's elbow, and then away.

I LEAN AGAINST a fence post, arms crossed against the chill. In contrast, Mr. Travis is warm from effort, his coat off and his shirtsleeves rolled up. His forearms are thickly dusted with dark hair. He chops wood with impressive energy; the little pile that was beside him when I first arrived has grown into a sizable stack.

"Mrs. Prewitt seems quite intent upon throwing you together with her niece," I say.

A noncommittal noise. I dig my fingers into my arms.

"It was *you* who introduced us," he says after a moment.

"At Mrs. Prewitt's request."

Mr. Travis casts me a surprised glance.

"She was most insistent," I add. "You were on her—rather short—list of eligible men."

He laughs, a low sound that vibrates through me. My fingers dig harder, until the pressure begins to hurt in earnest.

"You could do a great deal worse," I say.

He raises one brow, looks sideways at me. "I notice you do not say I could do any better."

"Do not look for flattery, Mr. Travis. It is beneath you."

He returns to his task, appearing absorbed, but speaks

again after a moment. "Despite her many fine qualities, I do not believe Miss Harmon equal to being a farmer's wife. There is a great deal of hard work involved—"

"How can you know what she is equal to?" I say. My voice is louder than I intended.

The axe falls with a thunk, and he turns to face me fully. "What does it matter to *you*?" he says, and there is something suddenly wild about his countenance. He takes a step forward, his hands tight fists at his sides. "Why are you so insistent that I consider her? Am I so—pathetic, so in need of companionship?" He swings away from me and then back again. "You are—I haven't words for what you are." His hands are raised above his head, the brim of his hat crumpled in one fist. Then he looks at me again. "You are *married*."

And there it is, between us for the first time. I stare at him.

There is an apology somewhere in my throat, but I cannot seem to dislodge it. Instead I stand with my back very straight, my chin raised as if to take a blow. I can feel myself trembling, but I hope, from the distance between us, that he cannot see it.

"I—" But I have no response, for I do not know why I am behaving this way.

"Well?" he says.

"I—I am your friend," I say at last, so quietly that I can scarcely hear myself. "I want you to be happy."

His face seems to sag, then, the lines that were drawn tight around his eyes and mouth suddenly slack, and he looks away. When he looks back, I cannot read his expression at all. "And you believe Miss Harmon can make me happy?"

"Yes," I say, softly. I am brittle, breakable.

He shakes his head. "I am not sure why," he says at last, "but I did not think you would lie to me."

Chapter Twenty-Nine

The leaves have completely fallen, and the air is truly cold. It is too cold for any sensible woman to walk out if she does not have to, and, as I am always—always—sensible, I remain indoors near the fire except when parish business obliges me to venture out with a poultice or tincture for an ailing cottager. Lady Catherine is particularly vehement in her advice that we must all avoid growing too cold at all costs, and so I do not mention my forays into the sharp outdoor air unless she asks specifically about them. I allow the cold to drive my feet, walking quickly on these visits to the cottages rather than lingering in the fields between Rosings and the farms, and though I feel a slight shock of anticipation each time, I never meet anyone on my way. I wonder whether Mr. Travis still walks out sometimes, despite the cold, on the chance that he might meet me, or whether he, too, feels the awkwardness of our last exchange. Though he comes to church he does not look my way, and I cannot say whether it is because he does not wish to, or if his seeming disinterest is merely a continuation of the game of indifference we have been playing these past weeks.

IT IS COLD enough that we have slaughtered the pig. It had grown so fat that we shall be well stocked with pork and bacon throughout the winter, with enough left to distribute to those less fortunate. Though Lady Catherine is generous with her tenants at Christmastime, some, especially those with large families, often require more food than she provides as the winter wears on.

I am glad that Lady Catherine's edict against going out in the cold prevents Martha and me from taking Louisa for walks in the garden, for I do not like to think of her reaction were she to run to the pig's pen and find it empty.

THE LETTER ARRIVES during breakfast. I am holding Louisa on my lap, offering her bites of toast, when Mrs. Baxter comes into the room. "Post for you, sir," she says. She bobs quickly and hands William a letter with a thick wax seal.

He drops it beside his plate, wiping his fingers and mouth hastily upon the tablecloth, then picks it up again to examine it. "Oh, my," he says, and breaks the seal. I lean forward, curiosity roused, and watch as he reads, his mouth falling open. Louisa wriggles, and I hand her another bite.

"What is it?" I say; enough time has surely passed for William to have read through the letter's contents at least twice.

When William looks at me, he is smiling in a queerly twisted way. "The best possible news," he says, "and the worst."

My heart beats desperately. "You mean . . ."

He fixes his expression into something more appropriately solemn. "My cousin Bennet is dead," he says, "and I have inherited Longbourn."

I am shaking my head. "When?"

"Not a week ago. Apparently he has been ill for some time."

I never was able to bring myself to tell him about my mother's letter. I look down at my coffee, growing tepid in its cup. "Poor Eliza," I say.

William's solemn expression deepens. "I feel, of course, for my poor cousins in their bereavement. But the two eldest made such fortunate marriages that they cannot be sad for long, for their circumstances are much happier than they must ever have dreamed they would be when this—unhappy event—took place."

"They have still lost their father," I say. "I must write to them. To Elizabeth, and Jane, and Mrs. Bennet." I look at him. "So should you, my dear."

William is already rising from his chair. "Yes, of course. But first I must go to Rosings—her ladyship must be informed."

He exits the room, shouting for his hat. I am left with Louisa, who lunges toward the stack of sliced bread, nearly upsetting my coffee.

WILLIAM RETURNS FROM Rosings Park flush with Lady Catherine's felicitations.

"She invited us to visit tomorrow," he says. I cannot help but be impressed that his enthusiasm for an invitation from her ladyship seems undiminished, whether it is the first such summons or the five hundredth.

LADY CATHERINE HAS sent her carriage for us. William spends the entirety of the short ride declaiming his opinions of her thoughtfulness and generosity, falls briefly silent as we are divested of our wraps and shown into the drawing room, and then begins speaking again on the same theme almost as soon as we have made our bows.

At last Lady Catherine interrupts him with a flick of her hand. "Do sit down, Mr. Collins, you are making my neck ache."

William bows deeply. "Of course, Your Ladyship, and please allow me to apologize for my—"

"Mrs. Collins," Lady Catherine says, turning to me and cutting William's words off entirely. "Your husband has told me of your good fortune. I am very happy for you."

"Thank you, Lady Catherine."

She inclines her head. "You are just the sort of person I like to see raised up a little in the world. You are modest and genteel, and unlike some ladies I could name, you haven't such fixed opinions that you do not recognize sound advice when you hear it."

There is nothing to say to this except, "You are too kind, ma'am."

Lady Catherine smiles and returns her attention to William. "I know I asked that you not remove to Hertfordshire until I had secured your replacement—"

"And you know, Your Ladyship, that I would never dream of leaving Kent until I am certain the parish is in capable hands. It would be unthinkable to do anything without first consulting Your Ladyship's feelings—"

Another wave of Lady Catherine's be-ringed hand. "Yes, you are most attentive to your duties. But I recalled this morning that I *have* heard of a suitable candidate. Lady Thornton wrote me recently of her nephew, who a short time ago received ordination. At the time, I said merely that I would tell her if I heard of a vacant living, but now . . ." Her smile is as self-satisfied as any I have seen. "I met the young man once, a few years ago when he was newly at Cambridge; he was most deferential, very pleasing in his manners. I wrote to his aunt immediately to tell her that the living at Hunsford is his, should he still have need of it, and if he does you may be off to Longbourn as soon as you wish."

"That—that is good news, indeed, Your Ladyship," William says. I avert my eyes from the confusion in his; to be so easily replaced must war with his desire to be master of his own estate.

"That is excellent news," I say, "but I do not know whether we may take residence at Longbourn quite as quickly as that."

Every eye in the room is upon me, full, in equal measure, of outrage and astonishment. William's mouth hangs open; I long to close it for him.

"Whatever can you mean?" Lady Catherine leans forward in her chair, eyes narrowed.

"Forgive me, Lady Catherine, I mean no disrespect," I say quickly. "It is only—the Bennet ladies will surely require a little time to make arrangements for their new lives? There are two unmarried daughters still at home, as well as Mrs. Bennet."

"And have they no relations to whom they might turn?" her ladyship says.

"Yes, of course they do—"

"Then I can see no impediment to your taking residence very quickly. They can have little to pack except personal effects, and no doubt they have long been anticipating this day. If they have made no arrangements for themselves, that is hardly your concern." Lady Catherine shakes her head. "I will send word as soon as I receive a reply from Lady Thornton."

Chapter Thirty

The sky, low and gray, threatens snow, but I cannot stand to be in the house any longer. It will be several days until I receive a reply to my letters to Elizabeth, Jane, and Mrs. Bennet, and I cannot seem to fix my attention upon anything mundane while our situation is so unsettled. A letter from my mother arrived not long after the letter from Mr. Bennet's attorney; she was suitably reserved in her effusions, but still I could read her happiness in every stroke of her pen. I cannot even say that being back in the neighborhood of my birth, surrounded by so many familiar and dear people—not least among them, my mother and sister—is unappealing. And yet I cannot rid myself of the sensation that I am suffocating.

A basket over my arm, I leave the parsonage, grateful that

William remains in his book room, oblivious to my movements.

In the woods, my footsteps crunch through the dead leaves. The world smells of winter, and all is still. I watch my breath puff white and ghostlike before me as I walk.

Mrs. Fitzgibbon's mouth forms an O of surprise when she opens the door to find me there, but she quickly urges me inside. "Here, Mrs. Collins, take a seat beside the fire. I will build it up higher—"

"No, no need," I say. She is wrapped up very warm, even here indoors; she mustn't waste good fuel on my foolishness. "Please, do not trouble yourself—this is perfectly cozy."

"Some tea, at least," the old lady says, and I agree at last.

The tea is weak but hot, and my hands are grateful as I wrap them around the pretty china cup. Mrs. Fitzgibbon settles herself upon a stool beside me and looks at me expectantly.

"Not that I object to a visit," she says, smiling, "but this is rather odd weather to be out in, if you'll forgive my saying so."

I laugh, feeling a warmth in my cheeks that has nothing to do with the fire. "I recently finished a present that I planned to give you over Christmas, but now I am unsure whether we will still be here then."

Mrs. Fitzgibbon looks startled. "Are you and Mr. Collins traveling?"

"No—well—yes. But we will not be returning from these travels. Lady Catherine believes she has found a suitable replacement for my husband, and so he and I will be journeying to Hertfordshire to take up residence at the estate he recently inherited."

"My goodness." Mrs. Fitzgibbon takes a sip of her tea. "Well, I suppose I ought to express my congratulations, and I do, but I cannot pretend I will not miss your company."

"I will miss yours, as well."

"You'll be quite the grand lady," she says, with a smile as mischievous as any of Louisa's.

I laugh. "It is only a smallish estate. But I hope I can help Mr. Collins make it more profitable than did its previous master."

Mr. Bennet always seemed to me an unforgivably careless master, preferring a life of scholarly pursuits to one of estate management. He rarely exerted himself to curb his wife's and youngest daughters' spending, or to deny their requests for extra pin money, allowing them to do as they pleased rather than disturb his own peace by subjecting himself to feminine fits of pique. And he assumed that Mrs. Bennet would eventually bear an heir to the estate, thus saving him the trouble of considering what would happen to her and to his daughters when he died—a grievous error in judgment that I will ensure William and I do not make the mistake of repeating.

I know very well how to publicly live genteelly while privately stretching pennies as far as they will go. William, of course, as master, will have charge of the estate itself, but *I* shall manage the household, and with a little thriftiness on my part, I've no doubt we can provide Louisa with a proper dowry. Though our income at Longbourn will exceed what we are accustomed to here in Hunsford, I have no intention of wasting our good fortune by buying baubles and bonnets every time I walk into Meryton. And with a suggestion here or there, cleverly disguised, I believe I shall be able to exert influence over the running of the home and tenant farms, as well, though if there is enough money, hiring a steward might still be prudent. It will all be something of an adventure, really; I feel the smallest stirring of excitement at the thought.

"No doubt you'll do well enough," Mrs. Fitzgibbon says. Her eyes slide toward the basket, which I set upon the kitchen table when I arrived.

"Oh!" I say, and stand rather too quickly. I reach into the basket. "I've brought you some of my mother's favorite blend of tea—she always sends some as a surprise every few months—and . . . this." I hold the picture up, unfolding it and feeling unaccountably shy.

Mrs. Fitzgibbon reaches out but does not quite touch the paper.

"Is that . . . ?" she says, smiling with something that looks like wonder.

It is nowhere near a perfect likeness, but I feel a little satisfaction in looking between her and the drawing and seeing a close resemblance in the sharp jutting nose and high brow. "I only drew it from memory—I should have asked you to pose, I suppose, but I drew it on a whim."

"It's beautiful." She tilts it to better catch the firelight and squints at the details. "Thank you, Mrs. Collins."

Embarrassed, I reach into my reticule and take out two pennies. "I thought perhaps you could send it to your sister— so she would have some idea how you've changed since she saw you last."

Mrs. Fitzgibbon shakes her head, grinning. "Oh, goodness, she doesn't need to know *that*. And I've never had my portrait done—I'll be the envy of the parish." She tries to hand the pennies back to me, but I shake my head, and after a moment she bows her head, smoothing the paper carefully against the table.

"Now, tell me," she says as we seat ourselves once more before the fire. "This new parson—what do you know of him?"

"Very little, except that he has only recently taken orders, and that Lady Catherine approves of him."

"Is he married?"

"I do not believe so; her ladyship did not mention a wife, and if he is so new to ordination he is likely to only now be able to support a wife when he receives this living."

"There now," she says, sitting back with a satisfied air.

"That is one good thing to come of your defection, Mrs. Collins—the neighborhood ladies will once again have the chance to vie for the affections of our young clergyman. It will be very amusing, I am sure."

IT DOES SNOW, but only lightly. I watch the flakes fall outside my parlor window until darkness hides all but my own reflection, and then I turn away.

Chapter Thirty-One

Mr. Bolton will be able to take residence at the parsonage in a fortnight's time," Lady Catherine announces almost as soon as William and I have entered her drawing room. We are both startled in the process of bowing, stopping halfway down and staring at her. I am sure we must look ridiculous, yet Lady Catherine looks extremely pleased.

"He is a very sensible young man," she says as we take our seats. "Lady Thornton assures me he is properly grateful for this opportunity."

"Two weeks, ma'am?" I cannot help saying. My mind feels shocked and blank, and my voice seems to come from a great distance.

"You cannot require more time than that to put your affairs in order, surely?" she says, brows raised.

"No, indeed, Lady Catherine," William hastens to say. "I have been in communication with Mr. Bennet's attorney since he first wrote to tell me the news of my cousin's demise. There is nothing to do but take residence at this point."

This is true; I know this is true. Both Elizabeth and Jane wrote to me in response to my letters of condolence, and each said separately that their sisters and mother would stay the winter with Mrs. Bennet's sister, Mrs. Phillips, and her husband, deeming the journey to Derbyshire, where Jane and Elizabeth both have settled, too treacherous for Mrs. Bennet's nerves during months when snow and ice are likely to make the roads slick. Mrs. Bennet herself has not replied to my letter to her, though I cannot say I am surprised.

There really are no impediments to our taking residence at Longbourn. I swallow, hard, and am silent.

Lady Catherine, apparently satisfied that there will be no other unnecessary objections to her plans, begins to speak of something else, and though I do my best to attend, my mind remains fixed upon thoughts of Mrs. Bennet.

My situation is no less tenuous than hers. I think of all those years she spent wishing for a boy who never arrived; if William and I do not conceive another son, the great irony is that I will be in the same position of relying upon my family's charity as I would have been if I had never married at all.

A few moments pass before I realize that Lady Catherine

has stopped talking; I look up to find her sharp gaze focused just behind me, her lips tightly compressed. I wait, glance at William, who looks uneasy; but it is clear that Lady Catherine has lost the thread of the conversation, such as it was. Slowly, feeling rather as though I am attempting not to startle a skittish horse, I shift so that I can look over my own shoulder, but I see nothing out of the ordinary, only Miss de Bourgh and Mrs. Jenkinson sitting on the settee near the fireplace, where they have been since before we arrived. The latter is reading silently from a small book, but the former has slipped into a light doze, her head falling forward against her chest as though her neck is simply too fragile to hold its weight.

I look back at Lady Catherine, and her eyes snap to mine, just for a moment. Her face is open and, dare I say, vulnerable. And then her expression sours in the instant between one eyeblink and the next. I drop my gaze to my lap and wait, quite still, though my heart is suddenly thundering away within my breast.

Lady Catherine once implied to me that she chose not to subject herself to the danger of having more children; she was fortunate that a daughter could inherit Rosings Park, and so in bearing Miss de Bourgh she felt she had done her duty to her husband and to the estate. At the time, I wondered how her ladyship's husband felt about her decision, and whether Miss de Bourgh's constitution had been sickly since birth, or if her frailty began after Sir Lewis's early death, making it impossible for another, more robust child to be produced even if Lady Catherine were willing.

Though, I suppose, were I fortunate enough to be in Lady Catherine's position, perhaps I, too, would choose as she did. She brought a substantial fortune to her marriage, much of which has likely been invested in the estate; being the daughter of an earl, she could only have increased her husband's standing in society; and she *did* produce an heir, however poorly. The argument could be made that she had already given a great deal toward the preservation of Rosings Park, and I rather admire her determination that it was unnecessary to give her very life, as too many women do in the course of bearing children. I've no idea how much affection existed between Sir Lewis and Lady Catherine, but I have a difficult time imagining her forming an alliance based on love, and so, presumably, a lack of relations between the two parties was no great hardship for either. But then again, I have a difficult time imagining her ladyship having much true affection for *anyone,* and yet the evidence of it was there just now, in her troubled expression as she watched her daughter sleep.

At last, her ladyship begins a new topic of conversation, and I dare to look up. Lady Catherine looks just as she ever does, but I cannot shake the stunned, stupid realization that she is a mother, as well.

FIVE DAYS HAVE passed more quickly than I could have imagined. With the help of Mrs. Baxter, I have been packing away anything that we do not absolutely need to use before we leave—there is not so much, really, for most of the things I think of as ours will remain here at the parsonage, ready for Mr. Bolton to take occupancy. I have also been visiting those parishioners whose needs are immediate, and the rest I will take leave of on Sunday, when William delivers his final sermon. We leave Kent the following Tuesday; William wrote Mrs. Bennet by express to tell her of our plans, and though I am uncomfortable with the idea that they have so little time to quit Longbourn, knowing that she and her daughters have refuge with Mr. and Mrs. Phillips only a short distance down the road made me hold my tongue. Mrs. Baxter will be grateful, at least, of the extra time to prepare the parsonage before her new master arrives.

Martha has been weepy since she heard the news of our leaving, and I have scarcely been less so every time I pass the nursery and hear her voice raised with Louisa's in some game or another. I asked her to come with us—the words rushed from my mouth before I could think, despite the fact that I had not even discussed such a thing with William—but Martha began to cry and said no, she could not leave her parents and her siblings, however much it grieved her to see Louisa go. I am determined to ask Lady Catherine for the favor of finding a new position for her, for without her wages, Martha's family—all those children!—will surely suffer.

IT IS OUR final Sunday in Hunsford, and the church is more full than is usual for this time of year. From my place at the front, I imagine I can feel dozens of eyes upon the back of my head, and I cannot help wondering whether a particular pair of eyes, dark and topped by disorderly brows, might be among them.

"This will be my last time preaching to the good people of Hunsford parish," William says. "As many of you already know, Mrs. Collins and I will be journeying to Hertford-shire. We are, of course, unhappy to leave you all, but are confident that you will be well cared for by Mr. Bolton, who will arrive next week to take my place. The Right Honorable Lady Catherine de Bourgh herself has selected Mr. Bolton to succeed me . . ."

My thoughts drift away from my husband's words and into less godly territory. I have not been allowing myself to think much about Mr. Travis these last few days, dismissing, with a violent shake of my head, those thoughts that did crop up, but I think of him now, throughout the entirety of William's last sermon. I wish desperately that we had not parted so poorly when last we spoke. I wonder whether he regrets it, as well.

The service ends, and I blink, startled by the sound of so many bodies rising and the din of sudden conversation. Because of the cold outside, only a few people leave; the rest choose to stay and visit, despite the close confines of the church. I am accosted by a number of ladies who want to wish me well and find that I cannot break free with any degree of politeness. I answer their questions as best I can, and accept their kind regards, and think, at last, that perhaps it is just as well, for what would I say to Mr. Travis if I did see him? What could I say here, in front of all these people?

At last, some of the women begin to take their leave, and I feel I can breathe a little more easily. William appears at my side and guides me out of the building. Just beyond the church itself, the churchyard lies cold and bleak in the thin sunlight.

"I will be along shortly," I say on impulse, and leave William to the business of seeing Lady Catherine and Miss de Bourgh into their carriage.

I open the churchyard gate and step through. Here is another thing I have not allowed myself to think on, but now, with our departure looming in only two days, I might not have another opportunity. I pull my cloak more tightly around my body and weave between the headstones until I reach my son's. But I can do nothing but stare at it; though I long to press my palms flat against the earth, there are too many people about for me to be comfortable indulging in such behavior. So I stand and stand, my feet growing numb within their boots and my body shaking. I have never been especially attentive to his resting spot, but now I am abandoning it entirely. I will never see it again. There will be no one left here who knows the tiny being sleeping beneath the soil. The thought is intolerable. I stuff my fingers into my mouth and choke around them.

"I am sorry," I whisper at last, and go, half-running to reach the gate. When I have closed it behind me, I cannot even feel relief that no one seems to have observed my farewell, so intent am I upon not allowing myself to weep.

I return to William, and we begin the short walk to the parsonage. He does not ask where I went, and I do not tell him, only encourage him to walk more quickly.

We have nearly reached the house when I realize the small figure in the distance, walking slowly with his hands stuffed in his pockets, is Mr. Travis. His pace is so slow and ours so urgent that we have soon overtaken him. He gives us one quick, startled look, then nods briefly as we pass. There is a pain in my chest, a physical pain. It expands with each of my inhalations, but when I exhale it does not grow smaller again. I look back to find him watching me, our eyes catching, holding, my mouth a little open, his a firm, unhappy line. I only look away when I almost stumble, William catching hold of my waist to steady me. My cheeks are hot as I murmur a thank-you. When I glance back once more, a little farther on, Mr. Travis is walking even more slowly, his eyes cast down upon the frozen lane.

Chapter Thirty-Two

Our final day in Kent is spent in such a flurry of preparations that I do not have time to think at all. Our clothes are packed and our trunks taken downstairs by John; Mrs. Baxter and I have left out only William's and my clothing for tonight, when we will attend our last dinner at Rosings Park, and our traveling clothes for tomorrow.

Louisa seems baffled by so much activity, and she goes to bed early, exhausted by being so alert to our movements throughout the day. I stroke her hair as she drifts into sleep for the final time in this cot, in this nursery. Tomorrow, though she does not know it, she begins her new life as a gentleman's daughter. I am glad for her, truly, and I hold on to that gladness as her breathing slows and deepens, and as I creep from the nursery and into my bedchamber and begin to ready myself for dinner.

"You are looking very tired this evening, Mrs. Collins," Lady Catherine says over the soup.

"I have been very busy, ma'am—"

"No doubt you have been too excited to sleep much. I can understand it, though I must remind you of the importance of a good night's sleep; you are becoming mistress of an estate, and you cannot allow tiredness to keep you from your responsibilities."

"Indeed, Lady Catherine, I have no intention of—"

"I remember Longbourn as being smallish, with an unfortunate arrangement of rooms, but it is larger than what you are accustomed to, at least, and I am sure with some guidance you will make what you can of it. No doubt your mother will help, and I would by no means consider it an imposition if you were to write me with any questions that you might have."

I feel very removed from this conversation; my voice echoes oddly in my ears as I say, "Thank you, Lady Catherine. That is most generous of you."

"You are magnanimity itself, Your Ladyship," William says.

Lady Catherine accepts our compliments with all the graciousness I have come to expect.

"You will be with your family at Christmas," she says. "That will please you, I expect, though I suppose you will miss the splendor of the holiday here. Still, I will send you Cook's recipe for rum cake, and that should cheer you. I cannot count the number of people who have sat at my table at Christmas and told me it is the finest they have ever tasted."

When the time comes at last to take our leave, her ladyship sends us off with much advice about our journey and with happy wishes for our new life, echoed listlessly by Miss de Bourgh. So many words are required to express William's gratitude toward her ladyship that it is another quarter hour before we are gone.

Though it is quite dark when Lady Catherine's carriage returns us to the parsonage, I look back through the carriage window to see Rosings's silhouette, even darker than the sky, soaring above us.

DESPITE MY TIREDNESS, I cannot sleep; my mind will not still, and my body is restless. I try to lie unmoving beneath the blankets, but it is difficult, and at last, fearful of waking William, I leave the bed and wrap myself in my warmest shawl. My feet in their stockings are quiet against the floorboards, and the door, well oiled, does not creak when I open it.

I find my way downstairs by touch and close myself in my parlor. The moon is nearing its fullest phase, and the room is washed in shades of gray. It is all so familiar: the furniture, with its dark wood and blue upholstery; the fireplace, cold now, the face of its mantel clock gleaming palely in the moonlight; the window looking out on the garden. I have already packed away the few items we will be taking with us: my sewing box, my books, the painted bowl from Elizabeth, and a rather amateurish watercolor rendering of Lucas Lodge, sent to me by Maria soon after my marriage. The rest will remain, and though I chose none of it myself, I am suddenly choked by the dearness of it all, even the carpet, whose pattern, blurred now by the room's dimness, has never been to my taste.

I sit in my favorite chair, legs drawn up against the cold, and wrap my shawl more securely around me.

I MUST HAVE slept a little, for when next I look out the window there is the palest light at the horizon, so faint that I know it must be an hour at least until true sunrise. My limbs are cramped and protest when I stretch them. I stare out at the lightening garden, where the plants sleep on through the winter, and wish that I could see it once more in the fullness of summer.

An old familiar urge takes hold of me, and I rise and leave the parlor.

Upstairs, I enter our bedchamber as quietly as I can. William rolled in his sleep and now lies sprawled across the entire bed. I remove my nightshift and begin to dress in the gown Mrs. Baxter left out of the trunk for me yesterday; I make it as far as sitting down at my dressing table, my fingers working to free my hair from its plait, before William awakens.

"What are you doing?" he says. His voice is heavy with sleep.

My hands still. "I could not sleep. I thought I might take a walk in the garden."

"At this hour? It is still nearly dark!"

"Yes." I have unbound my hair and now I am gathering sections of it to pin. On impulse, I add, "I might go a little farther, perhaps—I have enjoyed my walks here so, and would like to . . . say good-bye."

"We leave this morning!" William sits up a little more in bed. "Charlotte, I hardly think—"

"Go back to sleep, my dear," I say, and jab the last pin in place. "I will be back before you awaken, and long before we must leave. The carriage will not arrive until after nine o'clock."

He looks as if he might protest again, but I do not give him the chance, rising from my chair, crossing the room quickly, and opening the door. I do not look back as I close it behind me.

THE SILENT GARDEN holds no comfort for me. I walk the familiar paths, past the hedgerows and the dormant fruit trees, past beds of flowers I will not see bloom again.

I reach the edge of the garden and stop. Here, beside the lane, the roses stand sleeping as soundly as the other plants, their branches nearly bare of leaves.

Autumn, I think. *He said autumn was the best time, and I have missed that; it has grown too cold, perhaps.*

I could try anyway. A knife, I need a knife—

I rush to the little outbuilding where William and John keep their tools and find a small pruning knife. Back to the roses, my boots scattering gravel, but here I pause. I am no gardener, and I do not know where to cut.

At last I take the knife and grasp a stem between the thorns, cut it off, then move to the next bush, and the next, and the next, until I have cuttings from each. In my hand, they look like a bundle of dead sticks, and I feel silly even as I return the knife to its proper place and put the cuttings at the bottom of the basket I usually use for carrying herbs and flowers into the house. Then I hurry through the garden and out the gate before I can think better of it.

In the woods, the ground is hard and cold beneath a thick brown blanket of dropped leaves. My skirt rustles through them, the only sound besides my increasingly labored breathing. I move faster and faster until I am nearly running, the trees a blur to either side of me, my blood beating wildly, until at last my breath runs short.

I am accustomed to extensive walking but not to more vigorous activity. I stop, press one hand to my breast and the other against the trunk of the nearest tree. I wish we could stay here for another half year so I can see the woods once more in the spring: the ground lightly furred with green; the shy faces of the first violets; the gentle slant of the sunlight through the trees' new leaves.

I wish that we could stay forever.

I begin walking again, my pace quick but not so fast as before, and soon I have reached the fields. I feel strong and reckless, the grass crackling under my feet.

When I reach the last familiar hill before the Travis farm, the muscles in my legs are burning. At the top I look down at the buildings spread out before me, thinking of what I ought to do; it is an indecent hour to pay a call, but I hope Mr. Travis, keeping a farmer's hours, will already be at work outside somewhere.

And I blink, for there he is, walking up the hill toward me. My heart's rhythm is suddenly fast enough to hurt as it thumps behind my ribs. His head is down, and so he does not see me, and as he nears me I can hear him muttering to himself, though I cannot make out the words.

"Mr. Travis," I say when he is nearly upon me, and he lets out a startled noise and steps back, head jerking up to look at me. He gapes.

"Mrs. Collins! What are you—what are you doing here?"

I am intensely aware of the absurdity, the impropriety, of standing here at such an hour, but I swallow the apology that rises in my throat and say instead, "We are leaving today."

In the early light, I cannot quite make out Mr. Travis's expression. "I know."

"I . . ." I thrust the basket toward him. "I brought you cuttings. From the roses."

"The . . ." He stares down at the basket, and I am suddenly flooded with the heat of humiliation. I begin to draw the basket away.

"It was foolish," I say, speaking too quickly. "It was your father who would have really appreciated them—I do not know what I was thinking—"

He reaches out, his hand closing over mine around the basket's handle. My teeth click together as my mouth closes abruptly. "It was not foolish," he says, and there is a roughness to his voice that makes me uncertain where to rest my eyes. "Thank you."

"You're welcome." He releases my hand very quickly, as though suddenly aware of what he is doing. Though we are both wearing gloves, I wish he would touch me again. The thought should shame me, but I am too full of other feelings, just now, to allow shame any space.

I hand him the basket. "I did not know what I was doing— I hope they will grow for you."

He takes one cutting out and holds it up, squinting. "I think I can make it root," he says, and then he looks at me. "They will remind me of you."

I do not know what to say. The sun is rising higher, far too quickly. I need to return to the parsonage, but I cannot make my feet move or my mouth form the words it ought, words of polite farewell.

"I should not have been so ungracious, when last we met," he says after a moment.

I shake my head. "I was . . . I do not know why I said the things I did. I pushed you, and I . . . cannot explain myself." I do not ask whether he will offer for Miss Harmon, after all; I do not need to know.

"And when I learned that you were leaving . . . I thought I would not have a chance to say good-bye." He looks down. "I have been a coward. Even now—even now, just before I met you, I was trying to talk myself out of walking toward Rosings." A quick glance up at me, and then away again. "I thought that even if I chanced to see you, we would not be able to speak; and I feared that if we were, by some good fortune, able to exchange a few words . . . I would not be able to speak as I ought." He swallows, and I track the movement of his throat with my eyes.

My voice catches so that it is nearly a whisper. "What do you feel you ought to say?"

A faint, ironical smile. "I *ought* to wish you well in your new life. I ought to have done so long ago, when I first heard the news, instead of . . . But I am more selfish than I had thought myself to be. I did not think of your good fortune, but of my own—my own loss."

The words will fester inside me if I do not release them. "It is my loss, as well."

Mr. Travis reaches one hand into the basket and withdraws two cuttings. He stands holding them for a moment before looking up and offering them to me. "You should have some, as well," he says. "For your new home."

I reach out and take them gently. His words echo in my head—*They will remind me of you*—though I dare not speak them aloud. We stand looking at each other, and then I glance at the sky, which is streaked with pink and gold. "I must go," I say. "We leave soon—I should not have come. But I am—glad—to have had the chance to see you again."

Mr. Travis glances from me, to the fields I will travel to return to the parsonage, and back again. He looks as though he wishes to speak, but then he shakes his head. Now that it is growing light, I can see that he seems as tired as I feel, his eyes shadowed with purple, the lines about his mouth cutting deep.

"I am grateful to have known you, Mrs. Collins," he says at last.

The space behind my eyes burns. "And I you."

There is so much else I could say, but I touch my fingers to my mouth before any more words escape. From the corner of my eye, I see Mr. Travis lift a hand as though to reach out; then his fingers curl into his palm, and his arm drops back to his side.

Chapter Thirty-Three

I return to a house in uproar.

John is outside, busy piling our trunks so they can be quickly loaded onto the carriage when it arrives. Lady Catherine's generosity has extended to the loan of one of her carriages to convey us to the posting station, from which we shall catch a post chaise for the rest of our journey. John nods when he sees me but continues his work without pause; I remove my gloves and rub one palm quickly over my face. With luck, any redness about my eyes and nose will be attributed to a walk in the cold air.

When I step inside the house, I can hear William's voice raised in agitation. He is no doubt as much in Mrs. Baxter's way as Louisa, and I feel the smallest stirring of guilt; I should have been here to corral him into some quiet, useless activity.

I open the door to our bedchamber to find William fussing at Martha over the proper way to air the room before Mr. Bolton takes residence. He barely looks at me except to say, "Oh good, my dear, you are back—Mrs. Baxter has left some breakfast out, I believe."

I watch as Martha takes the linens from our bed, bundling them into her arms and listening without expression to William's precise directions about their washing. "I am not hungry," I say, though no one is listening. When I leave the room, I close the door behind me.

I LONG AGO determined to live my life not in noisy discontentment but in quiet acceptance.

There is no use exhausting oneself by railing against the vagaries of fate. Doing so leaves no room for any of the good in life—and, I tell myself firmly, there is much good. Outside the carriage window, I can see Kent's gentle hills. Louisa sleeps soundly in my arms, her body warm and sturdy. Seated across from me, William catches my eye and smiles his odd, stiff smile. I find that I am able to smile back.

And yet. There is a pounding at the back of my head, and when I look out the window again, all looks blurry. I keep my mind empty, away from useless thoughts.

"I do hope Mr. Bolton tends carefully to the roses," William says suddenly. "I ought to have told Mr. Travis to look in on them from time to time."

I reach with my free hand into my reticule, where the cuttings are nestled gently together, and draw one out, just a little, so that I can see the dry and thorny stem. There is a strange heaviness upon my chest. "I am sure Mr. Bolton will understand their value, just as you do." I keep my eyes focused upward to prevent any betraying tears from falling.

William shifts forward a little. "Are you all right? What have you there?"

I lift the hand that had been resting upon Louisa's head and wave it with what I hope is a careless air. "Perfectly."

"Are you certain?"

"It is only—I took cuttings from the roses this morning. I hope that they will root at Longbourn."

His brow creases. "Longbourn has its own rose garden, I believe."

"Yes, but . . ."

But William's expression has cleared. "How thoughtless of me—of course you would want a reminder of our intimacy at Rosings."

I laugh; it is a damp sound. "Of course."

William settles back. "You have a female's sentimental heart," he says, smiling, and closes his eyes.

My hands tighten around Louisa, who sleeps on. I think, just for a moment before I shake my head to banish the thought, of Mr. Travis's reaching out to touch her cheek; of the way he knelt to look at her when he spoke. I am plagued

by the shadow of *if only*. I was brave, once; I made my own
chance. If only I—

Useless thoughts, all.

My finger strokes Louisa's hair back from her forehead. I
will tell her, someday, about how I was brave; and when she
is old enough, I will tell her that she needn't sell herself as
cheaply as I did. That she must recognize her own worth,
whatever others say. I will do everything I can to make sure
my daughter has as substantial a dowry as we can provide.
She will never be an Anne de Bourgh, heiress to a grand
estate and able to marry, or not, at her own discretion—
Longbourn's entail has seen to that—but with a large enough
settlement she will have greater freedom of choice than I had.
When love finds her, she may choose it over prudence. And
oh, I will make sure she knows how to recognize love when
it arrives, even if it comes humbly, quietly.

Louisa shifts against me, and I prop her head more securely in the crook of my arm. I look out the window, where
the view is of fields lying quietly in wait for spring.

Beauty comes in many forms.

The carriage rolls on, bumping over ruts in the road.

Acknowledgments

I am grateful to many books that were incredibly helpful resources, most especially *Jane Austen's England: Daily Life in the Georgian and Regency Periods* by Roy and Lesley Adkins, *In the Garden with Jane Austen* by Kim Wilson, and *Jane Austen and the Clergy* by Irene Collins. A great big thank-you as well to Nancy Mayer for being kind enough to respond (and so quickly!) to my many questions about the fiddly ins and outs of Regency British life.

Thank you to my early readers, especially Emily Cahill and my parents, Chris and Abbie Innes. Your feedback was invaluable (as, Mom and Chris, was your encouragement to give up on a college major that would lead to stable employment and "just write" instead!). Thank you to my agent, Jennifer Weltz, for taking a chance on me and my book, and to my editor, Rachel Kahan, for seeing Charlotte's as a story worth telling.

And finally, thank you to my husband, Stuart Campbell— for spending countless hours listening as I read each chapter aloud, for your constant enthusiasm, and for your selflessness in encouraging me to take time to myself each week in order to write (even when things were more than a little crazy at home).

About the author

2 Meet Molly Greeley

About the book

3 Behind the Book Essay:
Why Charlotte Lucas

7 Reading Group Guide

Insights,
Interviews
& More...

Meet Molly Greeley

Stuart Campbell

MOLLY GREELEY earned her bachelor's degree in English, with a creative writing emphasis, from Michigan State University, where she was the recipient of the Louis B. Sudler Prize in the Arts for Creative Writing. Her short stories and essays have been published in *Cicada, Carve,* and *Literary Mama.* Greeley works as a social media consultant for a local business, but her Sunday afternoons are devoted to weaving stories into books. She lives with her husband and three children in Traverse City, Michigan.

Behind the Book Essay: Why Charlotte Lucas

It took about a year of once-weekly writing sprints to finish my first novel, *The Clergyman's Wife*, but the idea had been slowly germinating for a long time. I have, in fact, been thinking about Charlotte Lucas and her choice for more than twenty years, ever since I first read *Pride and Prejudice*. Back then I was ten years old, and with a child's understanding of what I read, my first and strongest reaction when Charlotte chose to marry Mr. Collins was complete revulsion. Mr. Collins was *gross*, and worse, he was a little bit stupid. Someone like Charlotte, who was friends with Elizabeth Bennet and therefore must be intelligent, would be miserable married to him. I agreed completely with Elizabeth's first reaction to the news of her friend's engagement: Charlotte had made a terrible mistake.

But time, and many subsequent readings, softened my take on Charlotte's decision, and as I grew up, she became the character in *Pride and Prejudice* who fascinated me most, her choice to marry Mr. Collins less horrifying than the circumstances that led to it. Charlotte had neither money nor the means to earn any, and she had no beauty, which was, of course, its own form of currency. Even when she was ▶

Behind the Book Essay:
Why Charlotte Lucas *(continued)*

young, the likelihood of attracting a
husband equal to or above her in station
was fairly slim, but as the years passed I
imagined the constraints of her situation
tightening around her like a net.

The truly sad thing about Charlotte's
circumstances, I realized, was not so
much that she married Mr. Collins
but that she lived in a time when an
intelligent, capable woman had only
two choices: remain unmarried and
risk becoming a burden to her family,
or accept the proposal of a man who
could offer her security, even if he also
happened to be a fool. Her story was
all too common in Jane Austen's time;
a woman married the most practical
choice available because a woman's
security, unless she was exceptionally
fortunate, was always linked to the
prosperity and generosity of the men
in her life. The remarkable thing about
Charlotte is that she set out to seduce
Mr. Collins—not with her body,
but with her attention and sympathy.
Rather than wait passively for a man to
notice her, she saw an opportunity and
took it, and in doing so, she took charge
of her own life in the only way available
to her. I felt punched by the courage
and, yes, selflessness of her decision,
for in marrying the heir to Longbourn,
she ensured that neither her parents nor

her younger brothers had to worry about her future.

We get so little of Charlotte's inner world in *Pride and Prejudice,* and I wanted more. Austen tells Charlotte's story mostly from Elizabeth's perspective, with a few interjections from the novel's nameless narrator, and Charlotte seems, above all else, calm, practical, and more than a bit calculating. But Elizabeth, as it turns out, is not actually the most astute judge of other people's feelings and motivations. So I started thinking: what if Charlotte was just good at making the best of things, even if she didn't feel as cheerful about them as she appeared? What if she was grateful enough for the security Mr. Collins offered her to be genuinely pleased with her new life when Elizabeth visited in *Pride and Prejudice*—but what if security was not enough to make her truly happy in the long run? What if she finally fell in love?

Some of my favorite books take well-known stories and delve into the minds and hearts of characters who were peripheral to the original. Charlotte has never felt peripheral to me; even as a child, I couldn't read *Pride and Prejudice* without having a visceral reaction to her story. It's a story about a woman's ▶

Behind the Book Essay:
Why Charlotte Lucas *(continued)*

worth, a woman's place in society.
It's about mothers and daughters,
because it's impossible to imagine
Charlotte's own worry about her
prospects as the years pass without
also imagining the strangling fear her
mother must have felt. And it's about
love, or the lack thereof, and what place
it would have had in the lives of women
who did not have a man with ten
thousand pounds a year waiting to
rescue them from the terrifying
uncertainty of the future. Such
women, like Charlotte, had to
rescue themselves. ❧

Reading Group Guide

1. Where do you stand on Charlotte's much-discussed decision to make "a very eligible match," as her mother puts it? Is she exercising agency and practicality, or making a terrible mistake by giving in to social pressure and fear of spinsterhood? What other paths might she have chosen?

2. "I found his manner at once endeared him to me and irritated me thoroughly," Charlotte admits about Mr. Collins. Did you, the reader, find him endearing or irritating? Both? Something else?

3. In the extremely rigid class system of eighteenth-century England, the Lucas family became upwardly mobile with mixed results: "I came to see my father's knighthood as less boon than burden; though it elevated the circles in which we moved—thereby elevating my own and my siblings' chances at rising still farther—these chances often felt insubstantial . . . paired as they were with a lack of money." Would the Lucases have been better off staying in the merchant class, living more prosperously thanks ▶

to their father's successful shop?
If he had not been knighted,
what would that have meant
for Charlotte's marriage prospects
in Meryton?

4. When Charlotte admits she cannot
   think of any men besides Mr. Bennet
   who read novels for pleasure,
   Mr. Travis replies, "But certainly
   there are many men who *do* read
   novels. Indeed, a great many
   novels are *written* by men; it seems
   reasonable to assume that other
   men read them." What did you
   make of this? What do you think
   Charlotte's creator, Jane Austen,
   would have said about that?

5. "It is hard to think well of men
   when they so obviously do not
   think well of you," Charlotte reflects,
   when she first met Mr. Collins.
   Do any of the men in this novel
   seem to think well of women?
   Does her husband ultimately come
   to think well of her? What qualities
   of hers does he value? Which does
   Mr. Travis value?

6. When Maria, the younger and
   prettier of the Lucas daughters,
   chose to marry for love rather
   than upward mobility, Lady Lucas
   tells Charlotte that Maria "will never
   live up to our hopes for her now,

and that's a fact." Did Maria make the right decision? Why does Maria defy her family's aspirations and happily choose to stay in the merchant class? How will her marriage be different from her parents' or her sister's?

7. The heartbreaking story of Charlotte's first child, Lucas, was all too common for women in the eighteenth century. How does that experience haunt her? How does Charlotte's experience of motherhood compare with the grim story of the widowed Mrs. Fitzgibbon and her six lost children; or Lady Catherine de Bourgh, who obsessively hovers over her only living child?

8. Charlotte tells Mr. Travis, "Not everyone has the luxury of waiting until love comes along." Do you think their friendship made her reevaluate her choices? Would she truly have married a farmer rather than make "a very eligible match" with someone of greater means and status? Should Charlotte have waited longer? Would you have?

9. Will Charlotte, with her plans to economize and carefully steward the estate at Longbourn, ▶

be a better manager than the late Mr. Bennet? How do her history and personality make her better suited to the job, even though she is a woman and far less educated than its previous master?

10. At the end of the novel, Charlotte says of her daughter, Louisa, "I will tell her, someday, about how I was brave; and when she is old enough, I will tell her that she needn't sell herself as cheaply as I did. That she must recognize her own worth, whatever others say." Do you think Charlotte regrets her decision to marry Mr. Collins?

11. What do you think the future holds for Charlotte and her family? What will her life be like at Longbourn? Where do you see the characters in this novel in ten years? In twenty years? ❧

Discover great authors, exclusive offers, and more at hc.com.